Whisper ISLAND

ANOLA PICKETT

SWEETWATER BOOKS
AN IMPRINT OF CEDAR FORT, INC.
SPRINGVILLE, UTAH

This is a work of fiction. The characters, names, incidents, places, and dialogue are products of the author's imagination and are not to be construed as real. The views expressed within this work are the sole responsibility of the author and do not necessarily reflect the position of Cedar Fort, Inc., or any other entity.

ISBN 13: 978-1-4621-1167-1

Published by Sweetwater Books, an imprint of Cedar Fort, Inc.,
2373 W. 700 S., Springville, UT 84663
Distributed by Cedar Fort, Inc., www.cedarfort.com

LIBRARY OF CONGRESS CATALOGING-IN-PUBLICATION DATA

Pickett, Anola, author.
 Whisper Island / by Anola Pickett.
   pages cm
 Summary: Twelve-year-old Primmy longs to be a Life-Saver and rescue folks from shipwrecks along the North Carolina coast, but in 1913 everyone knows that being a Life-Saver is a man's job.
 ISBN 978-1-4621-1167-1 (pbk. : alk. paper)
 [1. Family life--North Carolina--Fiction. 2. Mothers and daughters--Fiction. 3. Life-saving--Fiction 4. Rescue work--Fiction. 5. Outer Banks, (N.C.)--History--20th century--Fiction.] I. Title.
 PZ7.P552537Whi 2013
 [Fic]--dc23

                          2013005914

Cover design by Angela D. Olsen
Cover design © 2013 by Lyle Mortimer
Typeset and edited by Melissa J. Caldwell

Printed in the United States of America

10 9 8 7 6 5 4 3 2 1

*WHISPER ISLAND is dedicated to the
women of my family—*

*my sisters Mary and Louisa, our mother Ruth,
and our grandmother Nancy—*

each one as spunky and determined as Primmy.

Also By Anola Pickett

Wasatch Summer

PRAISE FOR *WHISPER ISLAND*

"Whisper Island is a compelling story set in an unusual time and in a very special place. That alone makes it a top pick. . . . Readers of any age will not only want to read more . . . but will also be compelled to learn more."

James Charlet & Linda Molloy,
"Keepers" of the Chicamacomico Life-Saving
Station Historic Site & Museum

"In rich language and compelling historical detail, Anola Pickett tells a wonderful coming-of-age story."

Sharelle Byars Moranville, author of The Hop

ONE

mommucked—*bothered*

August 1913

S hoo!"
I flap my apron at the gull swooping from one
corner of the kitchen to another. Finally, she flies outside. That bird's freed herself of this place, just like my
mother nine years ago. She boarded the mailboat one
morning when I was three and never came back.

She's not given me much to hold a memory in: Picture
postcards from her wanderings. A little photograph
that shows her beauty. And the burden of a highfalutin
name—Primrose Estella.

I'm just plain Primmy.

My mother's leaving is a mystery. I can't fathom
why anyone would leave Whisper Island. This pretty

bit of land floats off the North Carolina coast between the Atlantic Ocean and the choppy waters of Mirror Sound.

Now and then I wonder what my mother would think of me if she'd stayed. I've not turned out as fancy as my name. I surely don't have a fussy life in mind for myself. I plan to be a Life-Saver when I'm grown. Do shipwreck rescue like Pa and my brother Jacob.

My brothers snort whenever I mention this. "Life-Saving's a man's job. Hard work all day, every day," says Jacob. Edwin chimes in, "No time for the kind of foolishness you get up to."

Foolishness has its place, and I do my chores before I get up to it. Usually. Sometimes.

Now that the gull's gone, I stir the chowder I've made for supper and push it to the back of the stove. The wash is hung to dry. I'm ready for fun and it comes right to me before I go looking.

A mess of red hair pokes around the doorframe, followed by Will Cooper's freckled face. "Hey!"

"Hey yourself. Has low tide settled?" Will lives right close to the ocean.

"Near about."

"Let's go treasure hunting."

Will points to the side yard. "And leave your wash on the line?"

"Why not?'

"Some critter could drag it away. And what about your supper?"

"The chowder'll keep warm till I'm back." I snatch up a gunnysack.

"You sure that pot won't burn?"

I'm **mommucked** by his fussing. "My chores are done. I'm going to the beach. Come along if you want."

Will follows me down the steps.

We've gone a short way when Emory Sperry jumps onto the path. "Where you going? Kin I come?"

Though Emory's only ten, I'm happy for his company. He agrees with me that every day deserves a portion of adventure.

We come to Cedar Point Harbor on the island's sound side. Near the fishing docks we pass a ramshackle building. Gray walls give notice: WARNING! DANGER! KEEP OUT! A metal sign—*East Coast Clams*—hangs by one corner and sways in the offshore wind. Birds fly in and out the broken windows. Inside, the place is filthy with their droppings.

We bend our path around the clam factory and cross the island to the ocean side. The Life-Saving Station sits ahead on our right, its white lookout tower standing high above us.

Emory's pa is coming out of the station cookhouse.

"Hey, Pap!" Emory calls.

Mr. Sperry waves. "Behave yourself, son."

The steady *swoosh, shuss* of the ocean thrums like a giant's heartbeat. We follow the path to the Lavender sisters' cottage and race each other to the water's edge. Waves play keep-away with the cream-colored beach. Rush in. Scurry away. Leave curvy lines of foam behind.

I dig my toes into the wet, hard-packed sand close to the water's edge and breathe in the salty air. Emory runs in a zigzag line and I follow, waving the gunnysack over my head. A breeze floats it out behind me like a sail.

Will spots a clutch of gulls, and we chase them until they take off one by one. They settle farther out in the water to bob on the waves. Their hungry squawks fill the air. Suddenly, three pelicans appear overhead. One dives like a dart into the water, and the gulls cluster around.

Emory laughs. "They're wantin' to grab themselves some supper."

He's right. The greedy birds zoom in to snatch bits of fish from the pelican's mouth.

I've had enough of screeching birds. "Let's find us some treasure." I shake my bag at the two boys.

We move down the beach. I've learned how to look

ahead as well as down when I walk here. Pa says that's the best way to see what's waiting to be found. He's patrolled the beach more years than I've been alive, so he knows what he's talking about.

Emory runs ahead and doesn't *seem* to look any-where. Not up, down, nor sideways. He just runs lickety-split fashion. Suddenly, he stops and points. "Glory!" He dances a circle around something in the sand.

He's spotted an empty horseshoe crab shell, whole and unbroken, as if the crab had crawled away just a minute before. A true ocean treasure.

Emory, Will, and I weave around a rusted ship anchor and the washed-up remains of a lobster trap. After a time, I see something up ahead. It's red, and the afternoon sun makes it shine like a ruby.

"Mine!" I race toward the prize, not looking where I'm going. Suddenly my bare toe catches on a rough board that the sun has bleached to match the sand. *Drat!* Splinters and sand grind into my knee. My stubbed toe throbs, and I fight back tears.

TWO

fladget—*a piece of something*

The boys run up to inspect my injuries. Will turns the board and points at a bent, rusted nail. "You're pure lucky it wasn't this nail or a splinter of glass."

I shiver. Last year little Ginny Pratt was playing by the East Coast Clams building and stepped on a glass sliver. She wasn't allowed near the old factory, so she didn't tell her folks for fear of punishment. Those wall signs now make it clear that everyone had best stay far away.

By the time her ma noticed, Ginny's whole foot had swolled up like a puffer fish, and bad blood streaked red clear up her leg. Mama Lu tried all her remedies to heal away the fever and infection. None of her cures helped. The smoke from burnt wool did no good; neither did milk-and-bread poultices. Poor little Ginny didn't last out the week. Her tiny grave is in the cemetery over behind our village church. Ginny's funeral was so filled with sadness that I bawled all the way through. Her ma wailed hard enough that she couldn't walk out to the grave on her own.

At dinner that night, I asked Pa if he thought my mother would be that filled with misery if I passed on. "No way to know," he whispered and looked away.

My toe burns something fierce now, but it's not bleeding. I brush away thoughts of Ginny as I clear the wet sand and dirt from my knee. I pour handfuls of salt water onto the scraped places to clean them off.

By the time I finish treating my injuries, Emory has reached my red treasure. "Hawr, hawr!" He bends over my find, holding his belly and yelping with glee. "Lookee here what Primmy found."

I hobble toward him, but Will gets there first and joins in the laughter.

Pesky boys!

"You leave my treasure be. I spied it first, so it's mine."

"You kin have it, Primmy. You sure kin have it." Flushed from laughing, Will's face matches his hair.

That's when I see that my "treasure" is just a **fladget** of a shoe—the torn-off, raggedy leather heel of a lady's slipper. Not a treasure by far, but I pick it up anyway and stuff it in my pocket. "It may not look like much to you, but I'll keep it just the same," I huff.

Will grins. "You're 'bout like a fellow my granddaddy knew. When he saw two boots floatin' in from a wreck, he gave his old shoes away. Found out when he got home that his new boots were both for a left foot."

This sets the two of them off into more rude laughter. I roll my eyes and shuffle past them.

The three of us move down the beach. I search for the rest of the shoe or for some ornament that might make a shoe's heel look elegant and worth keeping. Emory chatters on about his pet rabbit, Furbit, and Will keeps his eye on the clouds moving across the island.

"Looks like storm weather's moving in," he predicts.

Sigh. Bad weather season's coming on us. Pa and my brother Jacob will soon be at the Life-Saving Station night and day, keeping watch for ships struggling in the rough, shallow water.

We keep searching, but nothing of worth appears, and soon the sun's light turns gray-blue behind a cloud, making it harder to see.

"We'd best go," Will says. "Your supper pot will be right dry by now."

I snort. "Don't you worry about my stew. If need be, I'll moist it up with some coffee left from this morning."

But Will's bent on worrying. "If the rain comes behind the wind, your wash'll be wet all over again."

"We'll be well home before any rain gets here. Stop frettin' so!"

We turn back toward the path that leads home. The offshore wind has gained strength and fights us as we push against it.

"Phew!" Emory holds his nose. "Something's burning up bad on this island."

"The wind must be blowing from Jake Moore's smokehouse," Will says. "Pa said Jake had butchered a hog to smoke for winter."

"Primrose Estella Hopkins!"

Mama Lu stands at the head of the path. She lives in the next cottage down the lane from us and looked after me when my mother left. She's done all my "girl raising" as Pa calls it. Her proper name's Miz Lucinda, but I call her Mama Lu. She's thin and bent-over and old enough she could be my grandma. She's always treated me kindly and fair. I love her dearly.

But when Mama Lu's deep, crackly voice calls out all three of my names, I know I'm in bad trouble.

THREE

begombed—*soiled*

I struggle toward her, my feet slipping in the loose sand. My heart pounds away as all the possible reasons I could be in trouble march through my mind. I try to ignore my throbbing toe and the burnt smell blowing toward me. Once I reach level ground, I stoop to gulp for air and stare at my feet. I know without looking that Mama Lu's gaze is bearing hard on me.

When I'm close enough, she clutches my arm. "Primrose Estella Hopkins, look at me!"

I lift my head and see her dark eyes squeezed into a fierce glare. The wind has tugged strands of long white hair loose from the braids that crisscross atop her head.

"This just beats all, girl! Your pa's come home to find a right grim mess waitin' for him. Where's the sense you were born with?" She shakes her head so fast and hard that I worry it might snap off and roll to the ground. Then I shake my own head to clear away such thoughts.

A chill runs through me despite the August heat and Mama Lu's warm grip. Did I cause Pa's supper to burn? Something worse?

"First thing to greet him is a heap of sheets tore clean off the line by some critter and dragged through the dirt. Those sheets are thoroughly **begombed.** Wouldn't have happened if you'd been where you should'a been this afternoon."

Will snickers behind me. "Told you so."

If I weren't already in trouble, I'd turn around and kick him. Hard.

"Sorry, ma'am," I say.

"Sorry's a right nice word, Primrose Hopkins, but it won't fix things. Lucky for you I came by to see if you'd help put up a batch of cactus jelly in the morning. I smelled that stewpot from clear over in my own kitchen. Went in and pulled it off the stove, but I left the tangle of muddy sheets for you."

"Thank you, ma'am." I hope that using some of the polite words Mama Lu has taught me shows her my regret.

Her grip on my arm eases up some. "You'd best get home now. Your pa and brothers'll be wanting their supper." She shakes her head. "I thought you were turning onto the road toward being a woman, but here you are, still lollygagging along on a child's path."

I tense up, stiff as a fence post, ready for what's surely coming next: a lecture about how I should be learning all the ways to be a good wife and mother. I have a more exciting life in mind for myself.

I'm a mite surprised when she just shrugs. "Now go make things right." She sets her walking stick firm on the path. The staff is as crooked as she is, and she uses it like an oar, pushing herself along the sandy path. "Come along, come along."

"Yes'm." I lose my breath trying to keep up with her, and I can hear the two boys panting behind me.

Emory grabs his shell treasure out of my gunnysack and makes his escape. "See y'all tomorrow. 'Bye, Miz Lucinda." He disappears off the path as fast as a ghost crab scrambling into the sand. His bare feet slap loud against the hard ground as he cuts through the woods. He wants no part of my trouble.

Will doesn't follow Emory's example. He keeps close behind me. I know he's only tagging along to see how bad my mistake is and what trouble it will cause me. If he has a chance, he'll be happy to tell Pa he tried to warn me about leaving the stewpot and wash.

I don't need a nosy boy adding to my misery. "Go home, Will." I whisper my command so that Mama Lu won't hear and chide me for being rude.

"Don't want to." He grins. "This is more fun than looking for treasure."

My fists clench. I surely want to punch him!

By now we're just a short ways from my cottage when Mama Lu comes to my rescue.

"Will, your ma will be wondering where you've gone to. Must be near your suppertime." She shakes her stick in his direction. "Get on home now."

Will doesn't move right off, but he's smart enough not to put what he wants ahead of Miz Lucinda's orders. "Yes'm." He turns and runs down the lane toward his home.

Mama Lu and I stop in front of my cottage. Crumpled heaps of wash clutter the yard. Ripped places and splotches of white bird droppings stand out against the brown mud stains. *Probably from that blasted gull!* I sigh. Besides washing everything over again, I'll have to patch the tears and scrub those droppings with vinegar.

"Here's your girl, Sam," Mama Lu yells toward the front door and then turns to me. "We'll leave the jelly-making for a later day. You'll be busy tomorrow with mending and washing. Now go inside and make things right." She hobbles away, leaving me to face Pa on my own.

The door opens, and my father steps out onto the porch. Some say he's the biggest man on this island. I believe that must be true.

A chill runs through me when I see the angry look on his face.

FOUR

addle—*confuse*

Hurry on, girl. You've three hungry men wait-ing for their supper." He turns and stomps back inside before I can answer.

His manner **addles** me. Anger doesn't often come to my father, even when he finds me the most vexsome.

Though all the windows are open, the sharp air inside our cottage makes me cough. Left-behind smoke moves upward, marking a line between clear and gray. Something else hangs heavy in the air. Something unseen. My brothers Jacob and Edwin sit at the table, hunched over mugs of coffee. I wait for one of them to tease me about the stew. Strange for them, they're both quiet.

Pa pours himself a mug of coffee and sinks into his rocker by the window. Once settled, he lights his pipe and stares out at the yard. The grim frown has not left his face.

The rocker creaks against the wood floor, the only sound to break the room's silence.

Finally, Edwin looks up. "Guess your stew's good and done, Primmy. Can't say as much for our sheets, though. I pity the poor fella who marries you."

"Leave the girl be," Pa snaps. "She's got work to do, mixing up a batch of cornbread and putting that stew right so's we can stomach it." He frowns at me. "Get busy now, Primmy."

"Ain't you gonna punish her, Pa?" Jacob asks.

"Spending the day repairing those sheets will be punishment enough. She'll have no time to be meandering along the beach. Right, Primmy?"

"Yes, Pa." I gather up the makings for cornbread and mix it in a fury. The oven is good and hot, and I give the bread over to its care. Next, I inspect the stew pot with a spoon. The bottom feels too crusty and hard to save, so I pour the top layers into a smaller pot. Butter and milk soften it up, and I set it on the stove.

While the cornbread bakes, I go outside to gather up the damaged wash. Pa follows me.

"Primmy, sure as anything, we should have named you Anne Bonny."

He's forever comparing me to the woman pirate

who sailed our waters during Blackbeard's time. Pa holds that Anne Bonny must have been a wild and careless girl. Like me. Although I have no desire to end up a pirate.

I plan to be a Life-Saver.

Whenever I mention my dream, Jacob starts his teasing. "A Life-Saver, huh? Don't you reckon that'll be hard, seeing as how you're a girl? Females aren't fit for surfman's work. Takes a strong man to pull folks ashore from a wreck."

This remark always provokes my bragging side. "I'm as strong as you."

Whereupon Jacob snorts. "Prove it, little sister."

Each time this leads to an arm wrestling contest, in which Jacob comes out the victor. But one day I'll get the best of him.

Just now, I need to show Pa how sorry I am about the mess I've caused. But before I can get to apologizing, he tells me some startling news.

"Primmy, word's come that Keeper Monroe has taken bad ill. He's got to stay on in Virginia until he's well."

It's hard to imagine any illness that would dare settle on the strapping man who runs the Whisper Island Life-Saving Station.

"Some things have to change," Pa goes on. "Since I'm the number one Surfman, I'll act as Keeper. It's time for me to move back to the station full-time for the storm season. I'll go in the morning with Jacob. Joe Britten and John Hutchins will move in tonight. Emory's pa has already settled in, along with Matt and Eli Stiles." Now I understand why Pa's so solemn.

Then he adds, "You and Edwin will stay here."

My mind races along, trying to catch up with all this news. "Why can't we go with you? If we're the Keeper's family now, we're entitled to live at the station."

"Herbert Monroe is the Keeper, missy. I'm just filling in. Best that you stay right here. Look after the house and animals. Cook and take care of things while Edwin is out with the fishing boats. Miz Lucinda'll keep an eye on you."

"If I moved to the station, I wouldn't need an eye kept on me!" I fire back. "It's not fair that you and Jacob get to live by the water and leave me and Edwin stuck inland."

Pa guffaws. "It's not like you're miles away, Primmy. Whisper Island's pretty near narrow enough that you can walk any direction to the water sooner'n you can count to one hundred."

I jut my chin out and muster up a fierce frown. "It's not right. You're leaving me behind just because I'm a girl."

"Watch your sassing, Primrose. I have enough worry

without a sharp-tongued girl snapping at me." Pa sweeps his arm toward the dirty sheets. "You'd best get those bundled up and inside afore some new calamity happens to 'em."

Hands planted firm on my hips, I don't move. I'm walking on the edge of trouble, but I don't care.

"Primmy, I'm plumb out of patience with you. Get a move on. Now!" Pa slaps the porch railing.

"Yessir." I scurry around the yard, stuff the mess into a gunnysack, and start up the steps.

Pa waits on the porch bench. "Sit here with me for a minute." His voice has gentled, but his frown digs in deeper. He sighs. "One more thing, Primmy, afore you go in. The mailboat brought this for you."

He reaches in his shirt pocket and hands over a square pink envelope. My name is written across the front. I've seen the deep blue ink and lacy script before.

It is my mother's handwriting.

FIVE

taradiddle—*pretentious, silly talk or writing*

The paper weighs heavy in my hand. I turn the envelope over and see *Rose Alene Whitney Hopkins* printed across the flap. My mother's never sent me a real letter, just big city, **taradiddle** postcard messages: "Having a superb visit in this beautiful place." Not one word about how she hoped I was doing all right or that she was sending me her love. Nothing like you'd expect a mother to write to her only child.

Far as I know, she's never written to Pa. Of course, no word to Jacob and Edwin. They're not her true sons, having been born to Pa's first wife, Alice. Her picture hangs on the wall over Pa's bed, and she looks to be right kindly and sweet. I wish Alice had been my mother too, but she died when Edwin was two and Jacob was four—long before I came along.

While I stand there staring at the letter, Pa takes the sheets from me. "I'll put this bundle inside," he says. "Edwin can see to supper while you read that."

"No." I stuff the envelope in my pocket and wrap it around the red shoe heel. "I'll wait 'til later."

After we eat, Pa and Jacob get busy readying for their move to the station. Edwin takes the supper leavings out to his sow, Pansy. I can hear her grunts of pleasure as I wash the dishes and wonder what my mother has to say to me.

When my after-supper chores are finished, I go to my little room curtained off the kitchen and read my letter by the light of the kerosene lamp.

> *Dear Primrose Estella,*
>
> *I guess this letter must be a surprise, but I have an even bigger surprise for you! I'll be in Cranston from August 18th through the 20th and would like you to come for a visit.*

I stop reading right there. I'll turn twelve on August 18th. Is she offering this trip to celebrate my birthday? Her letter ends without a mention of it.

> *I'll be staying at the Virginia Dare Hotel. Ask your*

father if you can come to meet me there and assure him
that I will reimburse him for your travel expenses.
   I look forward to seeing you then!
   Your loving mother,
   Rose Alene Whitney Hopkins

Those closing words make me prickly. My loving mother? Not seeing a body for nine years is a mighty peculiar way to show your affection. I stick the letter in my Bible next to the little photograph Pa one time carried inside his pocket watch. My mother looks out at me, and I slam the holy book shut on her smile. I leave her to spend the night on the wobbly bookshelf Jacob fashioned from shipwreck boards when he was my age.

I decide to talk over the contents of my letter with Mama Lu before I mention it to Pa. No point in upsetting him. I tend to my sore toe and knee and get in bed. Worries about my mother's invitation cause me considerable unrest, but I finally drop off to sleep.

Will's bad weather prediction was wrong. As often happens here, the storm changed course and left us with a calm night. Our rooster's crackly greeting wakes me at daybreak. I toss off my nightclothes, dress in a flurry, and stumble to the kitchen, hoping to see Pa before he leaves.

The first rays of light push into the darkness. I'm alone. I check under the sugar jar for messages. There are two:

> *Primmy, we're off to the station. Mind things and call on Miz Lucinda if you have need. Remember this is Thursday.*
> *Pa*

That's to remind me that Mr. Bachmeier will happen by for supper. It's his habit to be at our gate every Thursday just when I'm putting supper on the table. I sigh and read the second note.

> *Little sister—I've gone to have breakfast with Nate Morehouse on the way to the boat. Back for supper.*
> *Edwin*

I grin at that. Edwin's sweet on Katrina Morehouse and snatches any reason he can find to see her. He works on her pa's fishing boat, but he hopes one day to have his own. I suppose then he'll ask Katrina to marry him. That seems to be the way of things.

After breakfast, I go in to pull up the covers on my bed. My Bible stares at me, reminding me of the letter inside its pages, but I choose to pay it no mind. I've work to do. The day's turned sunny. Perfect for hanging wash.

I'm out in the yard rubbing vinegar onto the bird droppings when Will and Emory appear. Emory's walking Furbit on a rope leash like she's a dog. The furry critter twists and pulls against the rope. No doubt she prefers to be treated like the rabbit God made her.

"When'll you be done with your chores?" Will asks.

Ornery boy! He knows I have hours of work to repair yesterday's calamity. "No time soon."

"Kin we help?" Emory asks.

"No," I snap. "I've got to do this myself."

Emory's shoulders droop.

"Thank you, though." I try to make up for my rude manner.

"C'mon, Emory. Primmy's too busy to bother with us," Will says. "Let's go dig us some clams for your aunt to fry up for dinner."

Drat! Will knows I love clamming almost more than treasure hunting.

Emory grins and slaps his leg. "Hoo-boy! Clams for dinner." Then his smile disappears. "I cain't, Will. Furbit don't like the sand, and I promised Auntie to keep my rabbit out of her way while she digs a new garden patch."

Will looks at me and then at Emory, then back to me.

I know what Will needs me to say, but I seal my lips. If he wants something, he can come out and ask.

Finally, Emory does the asking. "Primmy, could I, uh, leave Furbit with you while we're gone? I'll bring you back some clams."

Against my best judgment, I agree. Besides scrubbing, mending, and washing a ton of sheets, I've got to mind a pet rabbit! I know those boys won't bring back any clams. Not without me along. I'm a better digger than the two of them put together.

I tie Furbit to the porch railing so she can nibble on the clover nearby while I finish undoing yesterday's mess.

Thoughts of travel to Cranston tug at me while I work, and I wonder if I will make the trip. The sun is climbing toward noon when I finish mending the last ripped place, no closer to knowing what I want to do. I pump water to fill the washtub at the back of the cottage and come around front to collect the sheets. As I gather them up, I gasp.

Furbit and her rope are gone.

SIX

hummock—*a grove of trees*

Drat! Two days in a row I've put myself in the middle of trouble. Now what? I can't wash sheets and search for a wandering rabbit at the same time. I consider my next move. Mayhap Furbit's headed for the Sperry cottage. I hope Emory's Aunt Marcelle has finished her digging.

Suddenly, a dreadful notion strikes me.

What if Mr. Bachmeier catches Furbit? He's always going on about how his German ma used to cook up a rabbit for *hasenpfeffer.* If he catches sight of Furbit, will Mr. Bachmeier try his mother's recipe? He seldom leaves his cottage, 'cept for a suppertime tour through the village, but today could be the exception. I picture Mr. Bachmeier sitting down to stewed Furbit.

I have to save her from the *hasenpfeffer* pot! The sheets can wait. I race toward the lane, but then I stop. Rabbits don't follow set pathways. They're more likely to plunge into the bushes and disappear, just like Emory when he's of a mind to take off.

So I push aside some low-hanging branches of a fir tree and step into the dark **hummock**, a jumble of toothache trees, loblolly pine, and holly. Emory lives on just the other side. I try to avoid the snaggly bark of the toothache tree, but it scuffs against me as I push along. Uncertain about how to call a rabbit, I yell, "Furbit! Furbit! Yoo-hoo, Furbit!"

After a time. I can see my methods have accomplished nothing 'cept a batch of new scratches. I turn back to our cottage and add to my toe misery by stepping on the sharp points of fallen holly leaves.

When I get back to our yard, I give up the hunt, gather firewood, and heat up the wash water that's been warming in the sun. My foot's on the porch step when I hear squeaky little whimpers and spot a patch of light brown.

Furbit is napping in the shade under the bench. Her nose and cheeks twitch as she snores.

I'm a mix of mad and happy. "Have you been here the whole time?" I clap my hands.

Her eyes pop open, and her nose quivers rapid-fire.

She sits back on her haunches, ready to bolt, but I step on the rope. "Oh no, you don't!" I tie her to a bench leg with a better knot and take the sheets to the washtub, where the water's heated up. I scrub everything hard with lye soap and then rinse it all in cold water.

This time, I use wooden pegs to pin the wet sheets hard and fast to the line.

After I throw the rinse water on my tomato plants, I give Furbit a bowl of water. I fetch an apple and a slice of cornbread from the kitchen and settle on the porch bench.

The day's sun and breeze dry the sheets lickety-split, and I take them down before some new calamity strikes. I'm inside putting things away when I hear footsteps.

"We're back!" Will hollers from the path.

"Howdy," Emory adds. "How come Furbit's on the porch?"

I sidestep part of the truth. "I thought she'd find more comfort in the shade."

Emory scratches his head but says nothing.

"Where are my clams?" I know full well they didn't dig up even one.

"Sorry, Primmy." Will hangs his head.

He seems so downright mortified that I don't have the heart to point out that he needed me along to have any clamming success.

Instead, I fix them some cornbread and milk. Before I swallow my second bite, they're finished.

"I'd best git home." Emory wipes his mouth on his sleeve and unties Furbit's leash. The two slip away into the woods.

Will stays behind. *What now?*

"Primmy, I'm right sorry you had all that trouble yesterday."

I frown at him, speechless. What's he up to? I wait for the smart remark sure to come next.

He surprises me with a shrug. "See you tomorrow."

When he's out of sight, I snatch up my mother's letter and rush to Mama Lu's cottage.

She sits in her porch rocker, stringing bush beans. As usual, her gray tabbies, Mortimer and Mildred, rest across the back of her chair, their heads perched on her shoulders like furry earbobs. She looks up with a smile. "Done with your chores?"

"Yes'm."

"Good! I reckon you've learned that wash can't be left to take care of itself."

"Yes'm." I show her the letter. "This came on the mailboat yesterday."

She puts on her spectacles to read my mother's words. "Land sakes! Not more'n a scattering of words from Rose Alene all these years and now she wants you to cross the

Sound and meet her at a hotel." She looks at me hard. "What does your pa think?"

"I haven't told him yet. He had enough worry moving down to the station this morning."

She nods and hands the letter back to me. "What are you going to do about this?"

"What do you think I should do?"

"That's up to you, Primmy. You're near grown and old enough to know your own mind." She smiles. "You certainly have an opinion about everything else!"

"But I have no firm idea about this," I insist. "She left so long ago that I've given up missing her."

"Then mayhap it doesn't matter if you see her. Or if you don't."

She goes back to her bean chore.

My sigh can barely be heard over the snap of each pod.

SEVEN

druthers—*the way you want it*

Mama Lu puts down her work and reaches over to pat my hand. Her movement startles the cats, and they leap down in a fuss of huffy yowls.

"Primmy, I'm not the person to decide. It's up to you and your pa. 'Course, it'd be best for you to set your mind on what you want before you tell him about this."

"But, Mama Lu, that's just it. I don't know what I want."

She stops rocking. "Try a pros and cons list."

Before I could read and write, she taught me how to make such a list. She'd hold up her left fist for pro and her right for con and raise one finger each time I named a reason for or against. Then we'd see which hand had the most fingers raised to show me what to do. Now I can write out such a list.

I frown. "But that's always been for little questions. Like what to cook for supper. Or whether to go to uppity Elspeth Thornton's birthday party."

"And those little questions were good practice for deciding a big event like traveling to Cranston to meet your mother."

"I haven't seen her for nine years!" I try to keep the whine out of my voice.

"True," Mama Lu agrees. "Makes deciding more complicated."

This conversation is not proving the boon I'd hoped for. If I had my **druthers**, Mama Lu would tell me what to do.

Before I can press her for more guidance, Mama Lu looks skyward. "Afternoon's moving on, Primmy. What're you serving Gustave Bachmeier for supper?"

My sigh explodes. "Oh, drat! I near forgot about him coming."

"Your pa expects you to set a good Thursday meal on the table."

True. Pa says Mr. Bachmeier is a lonely widower and that it is our Christian duty to treat him kindly.

"Ham, potatoes, and cabbage, I suppose."

Mama Lu nods. "Gustave'll like that." She stands. "Hold up a minute." She disappears inside.

While I wait, I ponder a possible pros and cons list.

"Here. Take this for your dessert." Mama Lu hands me a plate covered with one of her fancy embroidered napkins. "Gustave particularly favors gingerbread. Whip up some cream for topping, and he'll go home a happy man."

I thank her with a hug and leave.

Back home, I set the gingerbread on the table and put some salted water on to boil. After washing my hands, I peel potatoes and chop cabbage. Supper's underway, so I sit down to write out a pros and cons list.

> *Pro—chance to travel off the island*
> *Con—I'd be leaving Edwin alone for three days*
> *Pro—chance to get to know my mother*
> *Con—maybe she won't like me*
> *Pro—maybe she will*
> *Con—maybe I won't like her*
> *Pro—I'll find out why she wants to meet me*
> *Pro or Con—I'll find out what made her leave me*

For all these years, no one's told me why my mother left. Maybe no one knows. All I know for sure is that her pa once owned East Coast Clams. But before I was born, he closed it down and left on the mailboat. Four years later, my mother did the same.

Sometimes I wonder if leaving might be a habit that runs in families.

The pros and cons list isn't moving me toward a decision, so I feed it to the cookstove fire and finish my supper preparations. Because we're having company, I pull off my everyday clothes—Edwin's cast-off trousers and shirt—and pull on my school skirt and the one shirt-waist that still fits. I wash my face and feet for company, but I draw the line at squeezing my sore toe into shoes. Clean feet will have to do.

Edwin is at the pump trying to scrub off a day of fishing when Mr. Bachmeier trudges up the path. He reaches the porch steps and stops to sweep off his straw hat, bow low, and pant out a greeting. "*Guten Tag, Fraulein.*"

I bend my sore knee in a half-curtsy and answer with the German he has taught me. "*Guten Tag, Herr* Bachmeier."

"And how are you today, *Klöbchen?*"

I frown. His German nickname for me means "dumpling." Pa says I should take no offense because Mr. Bachmeier is an old man and means no harm. To my mind, it just shows that he's in agreement with those who consider me to be somewhat plump.

"Howdy, Mr. Bachmeier," Edwin shouts as he rounds the corner of the house. He's pulled on the clean shirt I left for him by the pump. Edwin doesn't hold with speaking a language other than the one he grew up with, but he extends his hand.

"Howdy, Edwin." Mr. Bachmeier smiles.

The two men shake hands and step into the cottage.

"I heard about Keeper Monroe." Our guest sits down at the table and reaches for the bowl of cabbage and potatoes. "Now your father will be acting Keeper?"

"Yessir, least until Mr. Monroe is back," Edwin replies around a mouthful of ham. "He and Jacob moved back to the station this morning."

Mr. Bachmeier nods and prepares to take his first bite of the supper I've made special for him. When I was little, I used to marvel at how he'd smooth back his long, bushy moustache before each slurp of soup or chomp of meat. But this peculiar habit has long since lost its charm. He goes at his food like eating is a serious labor. Though he says little through a meal, his eating noise makes up for any lack of speech.

Edwin and I down our food without much talking too. If Pa and Jacob were here, the four of us would carry on a conversation. But there are only the two of us against Mr. Bachmeier's racket, so we finish our supper more or less speechless.

I serve up the gingerbread and coffee, and our guest makes short work of both. He pats his belly and rises to leave.

"Danke," he rumbles as he plants his hat back atop his abundant white hair.

I step outside with him. "Off veedershun."

He bows. "Good try, *Klöbchen! Auf Wiedersehen.*"

Partway down the steps, he turns with a serious look. "Think with care about your mother's letter."

EIGHT

call the mail over—*distribute the mail*

H err Bachmeier, wait!" I scramble down the steps and catch up to him. "What do you mean?" No point to ask him how he knows about my letter. Homer Clackhunt keeps a tight hand on the mailboat tiller but easily surrenders news when he **calls the mail over** on Whisper Island.

Mr. Bachmeier stops. "A letter from your mother is important. Whatever she says, you must think about it. With care." His fist stabs the air. "With. Great. Care." He turns. "Now I take my leave."

"But, please . . ."

He bows. "*Bitte, Fraulein* Primmy. I mean no harm. Do not ask me more." He lumbers away.

Shaking my head, I go to find Edwin chopping wood.

"Mighty good meal you served up for Mr. Bachmeier. Pa'd be pleased." He splits one last log, and I help him stack the firewood by the door. Before I can tell him about my mother's letter, he lets me know he has plans.

"I reckon I'll go down to help Nate mend a net that got tore up this morning. Make sure you shut Pansy's pen good after you feed her. The latch has been sticking."

I notice that he's still wearing his supper shirt. He'll no doubt do more sparking with Katrina than mending nets with her father.

When Edwin's out of sight, I change back into my work clothes, stuff the bothersome letter into a shirt pocket, and step into Pansy's pen to throw our supper leavings in her trough. She grunts her approval.

Then I light out for the Life-Saving Station. I can't let Mama Lu see me on the path so soon after Herr Bachmeier has left. She'll know I've not had time to do the supper washing-up. She's sure to scold me for neglecting my work. I make it safely behind her house, although Mildred and Mortimer yowl as I pass.

As I run through the woods, I think about my mother. I know she's beautiful from the little picture tucked in my Bible. Soft blonde hair sweeps back from her forehead, and her nose is small and straight. A fussy wrap hugs her shoulders, and she smiles at a bouquet of roses. I look nothing like her. My hair's the same brown as Furbit's and frizzes around my head. My nose is too large for my face, and roses make me sneeze.

Past the woods, the twisted path leads me away from Cedar Point Harbor. I can hear the steady roar of the tide coming in. The weathered Life-Saving Station stands out in the distance to my right. Someone keeps watch in the lookout tower, and I strain to tell if it's Pa, but then I remember that the Keeper doesn't take watch duty.

One of the Life-Savers will be walking the beach patrol halfway between here and the Hook Cove station six miles away, at the north end of Whisper Island. If Jacob has that duty, he'll be gone a good while. He and the Hook Cove surfman will trade gossip and then exchange metal beach checks to prove they finished their patrol duty.

As I near the station, Pa yells to me out a front window. "Primrose Hopkins! What're you doing here?"

"I need to talk to you, Pa!" I shout back. "Can I come in?"

"No!" His roar is louder than the surf. "You stay put."

He steps out on the porch and slams the door. In a minute or two, he's at my side, panting and red-faced. "What in blazes are you doin' here? Is something wrong?"

"I have to talk to you about my letter." I squint up at him to see how he's taking this. What I can see through half-closed eyes tells me he's not keen on the reason for my visit.

He sighs and sits on the bench in the station yard. "What is there to talk about, Primmy? I reckon it's nice you heard from your ma." He stares out at the water.

"Pa, she wants me to meet her in Cranston on my birthday."

This gets his attention. "Cranston? How's she reckon you'll get there?"

My patience runs thin with grown-ups putting me off. I didn't come for questions. I have enough of my own. I want Pa to say, "Why sure, Primmy, that's a fine idea." Or, "There's no way I'll let you do that!"

I take a deep breath, trying to quiet my irritation. "By mailboat, I guess. Her letter says she'll repay you for the expense of my travel."

He mumbles something under his breath, but I can't make it out. Probably just as well. Mama Lu says I already know too much questionable language from living in a house full of men. I can tell from Pa's scowl that his words are surely questionable.

Finally, he turns to look at me. Even with riled-up feelings, Pa is a handsome man, strong and rugged. His sand-colored hair curls around his head, and his eyes burn blue against his tanned skin. He and my mother must have made a fine-looking couple.

"Primmy, if you want to go to Cranston to meet your mother, I'll be happy to provide your fare. No need for her to pay me back. I can afford to send my own daughter on a journey if I want!"

Before I can answer, Pa looks toward the village path. "Here comes your brother."

I follow his gaze, expecting to see Jacob returning from beach patrol. Instead, Edwin is running toward us. By the way he's shaking his fist in the air, I can tell he's mad, and I figure he's had a set-to with Katrina.

Then I remember his warning about locking Pansy secure in her pen.

NINE

goaty—*bad smelling*

Drat! I've landed myself in trouble again. I step behind Pa, hoping to disappear from Edwin's sight.

No such luck. Edwin's spotted me already. In a blink, he comes to Pa's side and grabs a handful of my shirt. I dig my heels into the loose sand, but Edwin drags me around to face him.

"Consarn it, Primmy! I told you to put the latch on tight. Now Pansy's tearing up every garden on the island. When I heard Adelaide Crocker screaming that a sow was eating up her leeks, I knew what had hap—"

I interrupt. "How did you know I was here?" My question only adds to his anger.

"Because half the island saw you sneaking down to the station, that's how!"

Even in the fading light, I can see that his tanned face matches Mama Lu's brightest red zinnias. Pa's grim look shows he agrees with Edwin.

I try to explain. "But, Edwin, I fed her right after you left, and I'm *sure* I—"

"Primmy, you ain't *sure* of anything you do. You just plow ahead and do what you want, any old way you want. Now come help me get Pansy back home."

I turn to my father. "Pa, what about the letter?"

He snaps, "What about it, Primrose? You seem disinclined to do what others ask. Settle it for yourself. Make up your own mind and let me know what you decide." He turns away and stomps inside the station.

Edwin still has hold of my shirt. "Let's go."

He pulls me so hard that I have no choice but to go with him.

A small crowd of village folks has gathered by the fishing docks. Will and Emory push their way up to the front line. Emory looks mighty worried, but the beginning of a smirk is stretching Will's mouth.

"Primmy," Emory whispers as I get near. "Aunt Marcelle is powerful mad. Pansy dug up the garden she just planted this afternoon."

I groan. Emory's aunt is famous for her late plant-
ings and the delicious root vegetables and greens they
turn out. "Tell her I'll help her re-seed tomorrow for
sure," I whisper back.

Then I see the Lavender sisters plowing through the
crowd.

"There she is," Hortense Lavender shrills as she
slams to a halt in front of me. The sudden stop causes
her considerable bulk to take some time to settle. "Do
you know what you've done?"

"No, ma'am, I don't," I foolishly answer. Of course I
know what I've done *in general,* but I've no ahead what
I've done *in particular* to Miz Lavender.

Her twin sister, Aurelia, thin as a fence plank, steps
from behind her sister to correct me. "Oh, yes, you do,
missy. You've let that horrible sow of yours ruin our
garden. Sister had a whole crop of Guernsey Half Long
parsnips ready to harvest and ship over to the Virginia
Dare Hotel." She whips out a lacy handkerchief and
bawls into its frilly cotton. "Now there's not one parsnip left whole and intact." She blows her pointy nose for
extra effect.

"I'm real sorry, Miz Lavender," I begin.

"Sorry don't cut it, girlie. You're a wild, spoiled brat!"
the larger Lavender shouts. "No wonder your mother
abandon—"

Edwin snaps right into her sentence. "There's no call for that, Miz Lavender."

My stomach churns, and I strain forward, fists knotted. I long to punch the hateful woman.

Edwin's hand twists my shirt tighter to keep me near him. "Primmy made a mistake and she's sorry."

Elbert Pepperdine steps up to pat my shoulder. He has a gift for making light of things. "Maybe you could send Pansy over to the Virginia Dare chef. She'd make mighty fine dining. Better'n parsnips!" He rubs his belly like it's full of pork roast, and the crowd laughs.

Edwin doesn't join in. "No, sirree. Pansy's staying right here on Whisper Island. Now, let's go get her."

He drags me away. We're followed by Will and Emory, no doubt looking for excitement. Do they think corralling a critter that surely weighs even more than Hortense Lavender will be *fun*?

We're headed toward the Lavender place when a loud yelp and a louder snort stop us in our tracks.

"That's Aunt Marcelle," Emory yells the same time Edwin shouts, "That's Pansy!"

We round a curve and come upon Emory's aunt holding fast to a length of rope wrapped several times around a live oak tree. At the other end of the rope, straining hard, Pansy squeals and squirms to get loose from the loop around her neck.

"Ya-hoo!" Emory's aunt yells. "Help me hold this critter. She wants loose in the worst way."

Edwin, Will, and Emory hold fast to the rope section closest to Pansy while Emory's aunt and I unwind the other end from around the tree. Then the five of us, sweating and grunting, pull, push, and drag Pansy back home. When we lock her in her pen, I get a strong, **goaty** whiff of Miz Crocker's leeks. We'll be smelling them for a few days, one way or another.

Trying to make amends for my latest misadventure, I bring out a jug of lemonade and pass it around our hot, tired group.

Will hasn't said a word ever since Edwin and I faced the villagers, but now he turns to Emory's aunt. "Miz Hoover, how'd you learn to throw a lasso?"

She chuckles. "Will, I wasn't always a widow aunt helping her brother raise his boy. My husband was a cowhand over in Texas till he got hisself caught in a stampede." She slaps her knee. "I ain't had this much fun since then. Almost makes up for my ruint garden."

I stare at her and marvel at all the things I don't know about the people who live right close. Emory and his family are Negro, and I'd never had an idea that any of their kin were cowboys.

Emory's pa is a surfman, and the Lavender sisters disapprove. They don't hold much with Negroes doing anything but what Pa calls "sweat and muscle work." I find the sisters' narrow view of humanity irksome, and it makes me somewhat pleased that Pansy chose their parsnips for her dessert.

TEN

lackadaisical—*in a careless manner*

After the Pansy round-up crew leaves, Edwin and I share several minutes of glummy silence. My brother stares at me across the table. I study the chink in the kitchen wall where I hammered in a nail last winter. I'd planned to hang a fine mirror that I hauled up from the beach, but the nail was too weak.

The wall chink loses its charm, and I finally look Edwin full in the face. "I'm sorry."

He sighs. "I know. You think you can do things any ol' **lackadaisical** way and folks will forgive you when you say you're sorry. You should know by now that sorry won't fix anything, just like Miz Lavender said."

I sit as straight as I can. "Maybe I can grow her some new parsnips."

"No!" Edwin roars. "You'd best stay away from the Lavenders."

I'm relieved to hear this, although I know I should do something to put things right. Maybe send Will with a batch of raisin cookies and a few jars of peach marmalade. She surely doesn't need sugary treats, but it's clear that Hortense Lavender favors them. No doubt she eats them all up before her skinny twin can get at them.

Edwin offers a more painful way to make amends.

"I'll stop there tomorrow and ask them how much the loss of their parsnip sales will set them back. Then you can repay them."

"What? I don't have enough money." I don't have *any* money is closer to the truth.

"Then I 'spect you'd better find a way to earn some. You're so all-fired set on being a Life-Saver, which can't happen because you're a girl. Might as well start now finding some other means to support yourself. You're too hardheaded and **lackadaisical** for any man to marry."

Now my brother sounds like the miserable Lavender women, although what he says is true. The Life-Saving Service insists on males. And I lack whatever virtues are desirable in a wife. Not that I care about that.

Edwin reaches over to pat my hand. "Sorry," he mumbles. "You still have plenty of time to grow up. You'll probably make a fine wife one day."

He's put more comfort than conviction in those words. No wonder. In one night, I've caused him to almost lose his prize sow and cut short his courting time with Katrina.

I decide to move on to what's bothering me. I clear my throat and ask the question I most want answered. "Edwin, why do you think my ma left me?"

My question seems to catch him by surprise. He leans back, studies the ceiling, and then sighs. "I don't rightly know why she left, Primmy." His frown is sad. "But I *do* know she didn't leave just you. She left Pa and me and Jacob. I was just nine—not as old as you are now. I didn't understand it a bit."

"But what about now you're grown?"

He shook his head. "Still don't. Not sure Pa does, for that matter. Leastways, he don't ever say he does. At first, he'd now and then say he wished he could have given her more of the pretty things she favored. But in the end, all we know is that she just up and left one morning on the mailboat."

I'm disappointed in his answer, but I don't press more questions. For the first time, I realize that my mother's leaving was hard for Edwin. He was only two when his own ma died of pneumonia.

He stands. "It's getting late, Primmy. We'd best go to bed. Things'll look better with a good night's sleep."

I go to bed wondering if anyone knows the truth about why my mother left. If I want the answer, it seems I'll have to get it from the person who left—Rose Alene Whitney Hopkins.

Instead of finding a good night of sleep, I dream of my beautiful mother. I reach for her, but whenever I come close, she fades away. The Lavender sisters weave in and out of my dream, laughing each time my mother disappears.

I sleep through our rooster's crowing, but bright sunshine wakes me soon enough. Edwin has left for the fishing boat, and I'm alone with a day full of fresh chores.

First, I pay a visit to Mama Lu's cottage. Mildred and Mortimer meet me at the door with a chorus of meows.

"Mama Lu? Can I come in?"

"'Course you can, Primmy." She looks up from her knitting with a smile. "You caused quite an uproar last night."

"How come you didn't come to see what was going on?"

"When I saw Pansy trotting by, I figured it wouldn't be long afore Edwin found out and took out after you. You had enough attention from nosy village folks, I wager. You didn't need me there as well."

I bend down to kiss her cheek, and she pats my head. The cats come to see if they can snag an end of yarn while we hug, but Mama Lu bats them away.

"What kind of mischief are you cooking up for today?" she asks.

"No kind. I'm hoping to make amends." I tell her Edwin's idea about the Lavenders' parsnip loss and the other plans I intend to carry out.

"Sounds like you have a busy day ahead."

She's right, but I want to tell her my decision. "I reckon I'll accept my mother's invitation."

Her mouth sets to a thin line. "I hope—" She stops herself and squeezes out a smile. "It's fine that you've made a choice, Primmy. Did the pros and cons list help?"

I assure her that it did, but I wonder why she didn't finish what she started to say. I don't mention my real reasons. To learn the truth. And stay out of trouble for three days.

ELEVEN

smidget—*small piece*

Will and Emory pay a call just as I finish putting the top layer of brown sugar and biscuit dough on a sweet potato cobbler. I plan to take it to Miz Crocker to apologize for last night's commotion.

Emory ties his rabbit up, and the boys step inside.

"Something sure smells good." Will reaches a finger toward my dish, but I swat his hand with a wooden spoon. I point to a **smidget** of leftover dough. "Sprinkle some sugar on that and we'll bake it real quick. You and Emory can have a share."

The dough's turned gray by the time their grimy hands finish messing with it.

"Is that cobbler for dessert tonight?" Emory asks. "I sure do love anything sweet potato."

"Me too," Will adds.

Hint, hint.

"Nope. It's for Miz Crocker. To apologize for Pansy's rampage through her leeks."

Emory frowns. "Hunh! Aunt Marcelle lost her whole garden. What're you making for her?"

"I'm stopping by this morning to ask if I can help her plant new seeds."

Emory frowns as his hopes for cobbler disappear.

"Next Thursday I'll make up a cobbler for Mr. Bachmeier's supper. There'll be plenty left for us the next day," I promise.

The sugared dough is soon ready, and I set it out on the table. It looks as if it could use a good dusting, but Will and Emory bolt it down.

When the cobbler is done, I wrap the dish in a towel to keep it warm and protect my hands. Emory unties Furbit, and the boys walk with me down to the Crocker cottage. I suspect they're hoping Miz Crocker will offer them a slice if they're extra polite.

Miz Crocker sits on her porch bench, enjoying a smoke on her corncob pipe. She uses two long hatpins to hold her topknot in place, and one is coming loose. She stands when she sees us on her path.

"Morning, young'uns." She smiles and motions us to sit on the bench with her. Emory holds Furbit on his lap.

"Morning, ma'am." I hold out my dish. "This is to apologize for Pansy ruining your leek crop."

"Not too much harm done."

Probably more harm to us who'll be smelling leeks for a while.

She chuckles. "That sow startled me, though. I think my screaming scared her off." She lifts the towel and sniffs. "Mmmm. Sweet potato cobbler. Bless your heart, girl. My favorite!"

"Glad to hear that, Miz Crocker."

"I'll serve it to Reverend Sewell when he comes to call this afternoon." She points toward the cottage door. "Put it on the table yonder."

I can almost hear Emory's hopes sink as I take the dish out of his sight.

After a bit of chitchat, we move on to Emory's place.

Aunt Marcelle works in her garden. As she whacks away with a hoe, she looks strong enough that she could have been a cowboy herself, and I wonder if the folks in Texas allowed girls to take on cowhand work.

She straightens as we open the yard gate. "Howdy." She frowns at Furbit. "Emory, put that critter in her hutch, please."

I start with some polite talk to open the way to my apology. "Morning, ma'am. How are you?"

"Fine as frog hair." She grins. "What're you three up to? You lookin' for some dinner?"

At the same time Will and Emory accept her offer, I shake my head. "No, thank you, ma'am. I came to help with your planting."

"Why, Primmy, that's right nice of you, but I think I'd best do it for myself. I'm pretty persnickety about setting in the seeds and marking out my rows."

"But I want to make up for what Pansy did last night."

"Well, now, let me think how you could do that." She points her face to the sky and closes her eyes. "Hmmm, hmmmm."

The three of us wait while she hums away.

Suddenly her eyes snap open. "Got it! When things start comin' up, I'll call on you to do my weeding. Nothing I hate worse'n weeds. And this ol' back gets tired bending over to get at those evil things."

I smile, but it's all for show. I hate weeding more than Emory's aunt could imagine. When I was younger, pulling up weeds from Mama Lu's garden was my punishment for most misdeeds. I swallow hard and accept her offer.

"That's settled, then. I'll let Emory know when I need you. Now, let's have us some dinner."

The boys practically knock her over getting into the kitchen.

As I close the gate and start for home, I hear her scolding. "You two go right back outside and wash up good at the pump. Those grubby hands are not going near any food at *my* table."

Good thing she didn't see what they did to that cobbler dough!

TWELVE

fetch up—*show up*

This afternoon I sit on Jacob's carved tree stump chair and ponder how to earn money on the island. I consider making pickles to sell at Mr. Pepperdine's general store but then decide against it. My last attempt at pickle-making produced shriveled bits that looked like green fingers left too long in the ocean. Pa tried one and claimed that his mouth didn't unpucker for a week. Pansy was happy to eat the rest.

Reverend Sewell often puts out a call for needlework to decorate the altar and other spots around our church. I think of answering his call, until I remember that the Ladies Guild members donate their handiwork. Besides, the scarf I knit Pa last Christmas unraveled because of stitches I'd dropped.

Pa was left with nothing but a snarl of crimped yarn.

Seems Pa gets the worst of my homemaker efforts.

I manage to stay out of trouble the rest of the day but come upon no practical way to earn money. At supper I tell Edwin about my decision to cross the Sound to meet Rose Alene Whitney Hopkins.

He frowns and studies his plate.

I wait, hoping to learn whether he thinks I've made a wise choice. His answer disappoints me.

"You oughta go tell Pa tomorrow, so he knows your plans. Make sure he's of the same mind."

I know he's right, even though Pa told me it was my decision to make.

Then Edwin lays another worry at my door. "I stopped in to see the Lavenders on my way home."

I shiver, sure of hearing no good news.

"Miz Hortense says her loss comes to three dollars and thirty-six cents. That's for twenty-one pounds of her fancy parsnips at sixteen cents a pound."

I gasp. "I'll be as old as those Lavender women by the time I earn that much."

"Sorry, Primmy, but I can't see any other way to make things right with them."

Friday ends quietly, except for scratchy hoot owl cries from the woods. I go to bed with no idea how I'll be able to pay for Pansy's romp through the Lavenders' parsnips. No idea if my decision to meet my mother is the right one.

Next morning I wake before dawn and eat a big breakfast with Edwin. We leave together and head to Cedar Point Harbor. The sun's first light shows wispy clouds floating through the pale blue sky. Near the docks, Edwin swings off to Nate Morehouse's boat. I cross to the ocean side and run along the water's edge, pushing the cool sand away with my bare feet. Gulls and terns squawk when I flap my arms at them.

Soon I'm standing next to the station stables and can hear the horses chomping on their morning feed. I poke my head in. "'Morning, Jessie. Hey, Lily. Those oats sound mighty good."

They pay me no mind, so I walk to the station. Emory's pa is nailing a loose shutter back in place. John Hutchins and my brother have opened the boat room doors. They're hard at work, polishing up the Lyle gun that shoots a line out to a stranded ship. The faking box sits nearby, the shot line neatly wrapped around its pegs.

"Where's Pa?" I ask.

Jacob doesn't look up from his work. "In the cookhouse."

I find Pa making coffee.

"Morning." I wait outside the screen door.

"Come in, gal." He motions me to a place at the table. He pours two mugs of the strong brew and fills mine half full with milk.

"I hear you spent yesterday setting Pansy's rampage right with folks." He frowns, but his eyes twinkle at the same time. "Before he went on patrol, Justice Sperry told me you arranged to pull weeds in his sister's garden. That's a mighty grand way to show you're sorry, knowing how much you hate that job."

Eager to leave the subject of Marcelle Hoover's weeds, I steer our conversation to my news. "I've decided to meet my mother in Cranston."

The surf's roar pounds into the silent room as I wait for Pa's answer. Finally, he nods. "Is this your firm choice?"

"It took me some thinking," I admit. "Mostly I want to see her because I can barely remember what she looks like. But I worry that she might not care much for me."

Pa slaps his open hand on the table. "Goldurn, Primmy, she's your ma! How could she not care for you?"

Then why did she leave me? I'm afraid to ask him out loud.

"If she'd stuck around, she'd see what a fine young woman you're turning into."

I can hardly believe my ears.

Pa goes on. "I'll arrange things with Homer Clackhunt and pay him for your tickets. She wants you to come on your birthday, right?"

"That's what her letter said—August 18." I don't mention to Pa that she seems to have no idea it's a special day for me.

Pa has work to do. Before I leave, he invites me to come have dinner with him at the station after church services tomorrow. "'Less a storm blows in," he adds.

I nod. It goes without saying that if a storm kicks up, there'll be no time off for the surfmen.

I leave and fly along the beach, scattering sanderlings on the hunt for a meal. Out of wind, I sit on a rock and close my eyes to think about traveling across the Sound. Will I be glad to meet my mother? Will she think I'm turning into a fine woman? Or will she see me for what I am—a chubby, frazzle-haired dumpling?

I've just raised my face to the sun to brighten my thoughts when I hear the slap of bare feet on the sand. Will and Emory **fetch up** behind me.

"Hey, Primmy!" Emory yells.

"Where've you been?" Will asks.

I long to say it's not really his business where I've been, but there's no need to be sassy. "Had coffee with Pa at the Station," I answer.

"Wish Aunt Marcelle would let *me* have coffee,"

Emory laments. "She says it'll stunt my growth and that fresh milk will put hair on my chest." He pokes his head down to look inside his shirt. "Not one single hair so far."

To make him feel better, I tell him that Pa fills my cup mostly with milk.

Will is still pursuing my whereabouts. "Where you off to now?"

"Nowhere special. Just sitting here watching the birds." No point telling them my thoughts.

They join me, and we watch pelicans nosedive one after the other for the fish those sharp-eyed birds can see from the air.

"Edwin says flying could give fishermen an advantage. They could spot fish and catch them from above," I say. "Just like those pelicans. I wonder why the Wright brothers never considered that?"

Will snorts at this. "They invented a flying machine, not a fishing machine!"

"But they flew it not far from here. You'd think they'd consider some practical uses for a contraption that travels up in the air."

Emory pipes up, "Pa says a surfman from the Kill Devil Hills Station took the only picture of their invention when it got up off the ground."

"Yup," I agree. "When it almost blew away, he helped save it."

Will snorts again. "You two go on like Life-Savers do everything. How come I never heard that story?"

"Not hearing a story doesn't mean it's not true." Emory puffs out his chest. "Surfmen don't help others for glory. They just do what needs doing."

I agree. When I get to be a surf*woman*, I'll be happy to work without folks making a fuss over me. Although it does seem that doing an important job shouldn't cut you out from receiving some glory.

THIRTEEN

mollycoddle—*to spoil*

There's no air stirring in the morning heat when Mama Lu and I arrive at church. Reverend Sewell takes Matthew 6:28 for his sermon lesson. I listen hard to the part about the lilies of the field and how they "neither spin nor toil." Those flowers seem right **mollycoddled** to me. It doesn't seem fair that they could just sit around being lilies and end up more beautiful than "Solomon in all his glory." I could abide in a field from here to doomsday and still just look chubby and plain.

Elspeth Thornton smirks at me from across the aisle, like she knows my thoughts are true. She's pretty and wears fancy clothes and probably never turns her hand to anything harder than a piece of cross-stitch. **Mollycoddled** for certain!

Church services let out before the sweltering air inside our little church reaches the boiling point. I've about whipped my cardboard fan to pieces. It advertises the Pepperdine General Store, though I can't see the need for Mr. Pepperdine to tell folks about his business. He's got the only store on Whisper Island. Where else can we buy flour or sugar?

I usually walk out with Mama Lu, but she leaves on the last note of "Abide with Me." Services went on longer than usual, and she has to get home to fix dinner for Mr. Bachmeier. His weekly round of meals starts at Mama Lu's Sunday table.

I decide not to hold Reverend Sewell's sermon against him. After the others file by to say how much they liked his preaching, I step up to ask if he has any work I can do for pay.

He smiles. "Does your request have anything to do with Pansy's adventures the other evening?"

"Yessir." I believe it's best to be honest with a preacher. "I need to earn enough to repay the Lavender sisters for their torn-up parsnip crop."

"Did you have a job in mind?" he asks, still smiling.

I hadn't thought that *I'd* have to come up with the work. "Maybe I could dust around the church."

He shakes his head. "The Ladies Guild takes care of that. Any other ideas?"

"I could maybe bring cut flowers to decorate the altar."

"Ladies Guild work."

I'm plumb out of ideas, and standing in the sun gets more and more uncomfortable. I squint up at the reverend, who's even taller than Pa.

The smile never leaves his face. "I *do* need someone to weed in the cemetery. I'd pay you three cents a week to keep the grounds free of weeds."

Weeds again! Did those lilies of the field have to concern themselves with weeds growing up around them?

Unhappily, I accept his offer and head for the station. As I slog along, last year's shoes pinch my feet. Walking barefoot on burnt-up sand would be even more uncomfortable, so I hobble along as best I can. Pa must have seen me coming because he strides down the station steps and swoops me up. "Can't have you limping along like that!" He carries me inside and deposits me at the table. "Now take off those hurtful things."

I sigh with relief as I release my feet from their prisons. Then I take time to inhale the wonderful smells of Pa's cooking. Today it's scallops, fresh from the ocean and fried in butter, along with roast potatoes and crisp green beans from Mama Lu's garden. Apple pie served hot with slices of cheddar finishes things off. The surfmen at

Whisper Island Station fix meals for themselves. Jacob says Pa's the best cook of all.

This is a day off for most of the crew, though everyone has to be on call in case they're needed. Matt Stiles is in the watchtower, and his brother's hoeing the garden. Jacob's gone fishing with a friend, so it's just Pa and me for dinner. While we eat, we talk about everything except my trip to Cranston. I'm not sure why Pa doesn't bring it up, but I'm too worried to mention it myself.

Instead, I tell him about Reverend Sewell's job offer. "It will take me more'n one hundred weeks to earn the money the Lavenders claim I owe them."

Pa's mouth twitches and he coughs into his napkin. "Primmy, it seems weed-pulling is your specialty."

I long to answer Pa with some of his questionable language, but I keep those words to myself.

After dinner we play three games of checkers. I'd rather play a running-around game like tag or Blind Man's Bluff, but I doubt Pa would care for that. I win two games, and Pa declares me champion for the day.

The front screen door slams. "Hey, Primmy!"

It's Jacob, back in time for the four o'clock beach patrol. He's near as big as Pa and sweeps me up 'til I'm looking straight in his eyes. "Burnt any stew since I saw you last?"

"Not one burnt drop," I sputter. "Now put me down."

He helps himself to a slab of pie and makes ready to start his patrol to meet the Hook Cove surfman. I walk a ways with him. The beach at the water's edge is cool and solid under my bare feet.

"Bye, Jacob." I skitter across the sun-warmed sand and walk over to the harbor. Skirting the clam factory, I take the shaded path to our cottage.

Somewhere nearby, a blue jay gives his alarm call, an angry screech to anyone listening. I'm about to stop in at Mama Lu's when I hear Mr. Bachmeier's gravelly voice.

"It's best that she go if she wants to, Lucinda."

"I reckon you're right, Gustave, but I wonder what Rose Alene has up her fancy sleeve. I've never trusted that woman, and I see no reason to start now."

FOURTEEN

dingbatter—*an outsider*

I freeze when I hear Mama Lu's poor opinion of my mother. Why didn't she tell me when I was trying to decide about going to Cranston? Why does Mr. Bachmeier think I should go?

I start for the porch. I want to stomp right in, ask why they feel so free to discuss my mother—and me. I'm about to step up when I trip on the brick edge of Mama Lu's front garden. "Ouch!" slips out before I can catch it.

Mama Lu bustles to the door. "Primmy, come on in. Herr Bachmeier and I were just enjoying some peach pie. There's a slice for you, if you want."

"No'm. I had a big dinner with Pa not long ago. I was passing by and thought to stop and say hey." I stay quiet

on the porch, looking in at the two old people who've
been talking about me.

"Come sit with us, *Klöbchen*." Mr. Bachmeier waves
his hand at the chair next to his.

I don't want to be unmannerly, it being Sunday and
all, so I step inside and sit at the table.

Mama Lu hands me a mug. "You look right flushed,
Primmy. Cold cider should set well."

I thank her and take a sip. I'm not flushed from heat
or from walking too fast. My face burns because of the
talk I've heard. The coldest cider in the world won't help
me feel better.

I sit with them, listening to Mr. Bachmeier's eating
noise, until Mortimer and Mildred wake up. They've
been enjoying their afternoon nap on Mama Lu's sewing
machine. They make a beeline for the bits of food that
have showered the floor around Mr. Bachmeier's chair.
Even though he smoothes his moustache before each
bite, several crumbs always seem to miss their mark.

"Meowr!" Suddenly Mortimer jumps onto my lap
and hisses at Mildred.

"Ah, *die Katze*, he is angry at his sister." Mr.
Bachmeier laughs and pulls the napkin from under his
chin. "She eats all the fallen morsels and leaves nothing
for her brother." He pushes back his chair and stands.
"I think it is now time that I go." He bows to Mama Lu

and then to me, takes his hat from the table by the door, and leaves.

When he's gone, Mama Lu walks around the table to sit next to me. "All right. How much did you overhear?"

My mouth falls open. "How did you know?"

"Girl, I've cared for you since you were a babe. I know every eye roll and twist of your mouth. Not much you do gets past me."

I sigh and tell her what I heard.

"Now you're worried that you decided wrong." Mama Lu states this as a fact.

"Yes'm."

"But you're also frettin' that if you don't cross the Sound, you might never have another chance to see your mother."

I nod.

"You might be uneasy about your choice, but you've settled on it." She leans over to give me a hug, and I rest my head on her shoulder. "I'm proud of you."

"What if she doesn't like me?" That one question won't let go of my worry.

"That's her loss, Primmy. Every soul on this island thinks you're a fine young woman."

I shake my head. "Not those Lavender sisters."

Mama Lu laughs. "Glory, child, they don't think

anyone on God's green earth is fine. Leastways not as fine as they are!"

I probably should laugh along with her, but another question bursts out of me. "Why don't you trust my mother?"

She sighs hard and puts Mildred on her lap. "Your ma never seemed to cotton to island life. Never tried, near as I could see. Seemed content to be a **dingbatter** 'stead of trying to fit in. Not much on keeping house or tending to you and your brothers, either. I'd been caring for the boys since Alice died. I guess your ma figured I could just add you to the brood. When she set her mind to leave, she went off without a care. Never looked back. She near broke your father's heart. Left him with three young'uns and a feeling that he'd fallen short of making her happy."

"But Pa's bent on helping other folks. Why couldn't my mother see what a good man he is?"

"It's hard to understand. Your ma loved him, but she wasn't cut out to be a surfman's wife. It's a hard row to hoe, 'specially if you're not born an islander. Too much time alone while your pa worked at the station. No idea how to raise up children. Mean weather to put up with, and she never seemed to get along with village folks. Rose Alene was a sweet girl but lacking in hard knocks."

"Why didn't you ever tell me any of this?"

"Wasn't my place. Anyways, you've made a decision on your own. You're old enough to find the truth for yourself."

"Pa could've told me. Or Edwin or Jacob."

"I doubt your brothers understand it themselves. Your pa saw no need to make you dislike your mother. 'Sides, I think it makes him right sad to dwell on it. He's happy to have you and the boys to fill out his life. He must have been as surprised as you when that letter came. Sam Hopkins isn't one to hold a grudge or take revenge, so he left you to decide. A lesser man would have hindered you from going as a way to get back at his wife."

I try to take this all in. I'm glad Mama Lu has told me more about my mother. I can't see why she found living here to be hard. Whisper Island is a beautiful place and friendly for the most part.

All that aside, Mama Lu's words haven't helped me understand how my own mother could have left me.

FIFTEEN

breeze up—*get windy*

Monday morning I get up extra early and send Edwin off with a big breakfast. After I slop Pansy, I go through the house gathering up wash. In my room I notice the Bible sitting where I left it last week. I open to the page I assigned my mother, and I look at her for a long while. I wish I could make her picture talk. I have questions piled up: *Why did you leave? Why do you want to see me now? Are you still beautiful? Have you met some hard knocks since you left Whisper Island?*

The woman in the picture reminds me of those lilies Reverend Sewell went on about yesterday. According to Mama Lu, my mother never spent her time spinning or toiling, and she looks splendid like Solomon in all his glory. I search for the page with Matthew 6:28 and slip her photograph into place.

While the wash water rises to a boil, I walk over to Mama Lu's to see about making the cactus jelly she wanted my help with. I hope for more bits about my mother while we work.

Mortimer and Mildred lie on the porch, enjoying the morning sun. Their eyes follow me as I come up the steps, but the cats don't stir. Unusual for August, the inside door is closed tight. Mama Lu never shuts out a summer day. I pull the screen door back and knock loudly. Once. Twice. There's no answer, so I push the door open a trifle. "Mama Lu?"

When silence answers me, I step inside. No dishes sit on the kitchen table. The stove is cold. I move from room to room. Everything's as it always is—neat as a pin—except for unkempt bedclothes. Where can she be? Monday's her usual day for washing. Mama Lu never lets a chore go undone.

It's not 'til I'm leaving that I see the note poking out from under her sugar jar. Spidery handwriting tells me:

> *Gone to Cranston on business. Back on tomorrow's mailboat. Primmy, kindly look after Mortimer and Mildred and feed the chickens. You and Edwin are welcome to their eggs. ML*

I stare at the words. Business? Mama Lu's never had any business that I know of. Other than keeping me in line. What sort of business could she have across the Sound? Whatever it is, she won't be happy if I neglect my chores.

"Come along." The cats ignore me, but I know they'll be around as soon as they're hungry.

I hurry back up the path and find the wash water's come to a simmer. I stir in some lye soap shavings, dump the sheets and towels into the tub, and churn them around with an old broomstick. I rinse 'em good in cold water, wring everything hard, and pin it all fast to the line. The day's **breezed up**, so everything will dry quick.

"Whew! That's enough work for now." I help myself to a dipperful of water from the pump and settle on the tree stump chair. I'll do the shirts and such later.

I'm just getting comfortable when Will and Emory jump out of the woods and into my morning.

"We're on our way to the beach," Emory says. "Wanna come?'

I'm tempted. Mama Lu's gone 'til tomorrow, and no one would know if I slipped away for an hour or so. I can do the rest of the wash when I get back. I wait for Will to caution me about leaving wash on the line, but he says nothing.

"All right. Let's go on patrol duty," I say.

"Naw," Will moans. "I don't wanna play life-saving games. Let's look for treasure."

But Emory's on my side. "Patrol duty! I'll be the Whisper Island surfman. Primmy, you be the patrol from Hook Cove."

We're well down the path when Will shouts at us.

"Hold up. I ain't gonna play like I'm a surfman. 'Sides, most Primmy can ever be is a surfman's wife or mother or sister. No such thing as a surf*girl*."

I snap back. "Fine! You can be our meeting place." That should suit him. All he has to do is plant himself in one spot. "Emory and I will walk three hundred steps away from you in different directions. Then we'll come back to—"

"I know. I know. You'll come back to where I'm standing and trade beach checks, which are *really* clam shells."

Will grumbles all the way to the ocean shore.

We post him on an old ship plank. Emory starts his patrol toward the lighthouse, and I set out in the direction of Hook Cove. I'm tuckered out by one hundred. Will probably still complains, but no one can hear, 'cept for the shore birds hunting food.

I'm about to two hundred when Emory yells, "Ship in trouble. Sound the alarm!"

This is part of the game that most irks Will. I run toward Emory and pull on Will as I pass him. "Come on! We've got to save the ship and crew!"

"There ain't no ship to save!" Will digs in his heels. "I'm goin' home. Helping Ma do her wash is better'n this."

Emory's gotten into the spirit of his alarm and wades out as if to a wrecked ship.

Suddenly things go wrong.

Emory bends over and starts hopping, his feet splashing the water something fierce. "I been stung! A jelly got me. Bad."

He makes it to shore, but it's clear he's in pain.

SIXTEEN

chunk—*throw*

Emory's yelps turn to moans. He's close to tears as he hops out of the water and drops onto the sand. He reaches for his foot. Two tentacles wrap around his ankle.

"No!" I shout. "Don't scratch, Emory. You'll spread it worse. Don't touch anything!"

"But it stings," Emory wails. "Get it off me!"

Will reaches him first. "Get him to the pump by the fishing dock."

"No!" I shout again. "Fresh water'll make it worse."

I grab up a broken shell. "Hold still, Emory." I carefully slip an edge of shell under the tentacles and pull them off my friend's leg. I **chunk** them, shell and all, far out in the ocean.

I turn to Will. "Help me walk him back to the water." We pull Emory to his feet. Drag him to the ocean's edge. We scoop salt water with our hands and slosh it over the deep red sting and tentacle marks. Emory pants so hard I worry he'll burst.

"It's just a little sting," I assure him. "You'll be fine."

The rest of Mama Lu's remedy comes to me, and I look to see whose cottage is close by.

The Lavender place is directly ahead. *Drat!*

"Will, go get us some white vinegar from the Lavenders."

"Not me! Get it yourself," he huffs. "This game was your idea."

Emory struggles between us, and his moans grow louder. Arguing will only eat up precious time. I give Will a fierce scowl and take off. I move so fast that I nearly skid into the Lavender kitchen before I come to a stop. Miz Hortense is sweeping the porch.

"Good heavens, girl. Where do you think you're going?" she screeches.

I blurt out the problem. She stops sweeping and holds her broom in front of her like she needs protection. "What's that to do with me?"

Bits of Pa's questionable language rush to my lips, but I swallow them down. "We need your help, Miz Hortense. If you could spare some white vinegar, I'll replace it this afternoon." I try to muster up a smile. "Please."

"Humph!" She slams the broom against the house and plods inside.

I'm unsure what she has in mind. Is she fetching vinegar or a loaded shotgun? Should I wait or run?

Before I can decide, Miz Aurelia's skinny arm pokes itself out the door. "Sister says to take this and bring it back full by tomorrow morning." She pushes a jug at me.

Grateful she doesn't lecture me, I grab the jug. "Thank you, ma'am."

I scuttle back and pour every last drop of that vinegar over Emory's foot and leg.

Bit by bit, his breathing slows down to a regular sound. I drape Emory's left arm around my shoulder, and Will takes the right. The three of us hobble toward the Sperry cottage. On the way, we pass the Lavenders' place. Miz Aurelia waits on the porch, wringing her hands in her apron.

"Much obliged," I tell her. "It eased his pain."

"See you return our jug." She steps away from the door and leans over to whisper. "Be sure not to bandage it up 'cause it'll make the pizen spread. More vinegar's the ticket. Now get him home to his aunt."

"Yes, ma'am," Will says, all polite.

As we move on down the path, we hear Miz Hortense.

"Aurelia, are you talking to those scalawags? Come inside this minute!"

Almost as if she knows something is amiss, Aunt Marcelle stands by her front gate. She stares at Emory's foot. "You young'uns don't have one ounce of sense amongst the three of you. Emory, you know to look when you go in the water. Just like your mama. She always had a hard time with the jellies." She shakes her head and helps Emory up the steps. "You two run along. Emory's had enough of your company for today, I do believe."

"See you tomorrow!" Will calls as Emory disappears inside.

"Mayhap." Aunt Marcelle slams the door on anything else we have to say.

We turn down the path, and Will pokes me. Hard.

"See what you've done. Emory's aunt probably won't let him go off with us, seein' as how you almost got him killed."

"Killed? He got a jelly sting, not a shark bite. That could have happened if we'd been treasure hunting. 'Sides, we did just what Mama Lu would've done to fix things. Emory'll be fine. Your plain water plan would have made things worse."

Will pokes me again and runs into the woods toward his house without so much as a by-your-leave.

Mad as he is, there's no point me chasing after him. I walk on by myself. "Good riddance," I tell Mildred and Mortimer as I pass Mama Lu's. I wonder again what sort of business she has in Cranston. Why didn't she tell me that she was going off like that?

The cats must be lonely because they follow me home. Pansy trots over to the fence and grunts at me, no doubt hoping for food.

Before I heat water to do the rest of the wash, I take care of what's left of my flower garden. Furbit helped herself to some plants last week, but a good stand of marigolds brightens up a patch by the porch steps. I fetch a bucket of water from the washtub and slosh it onto the yellow flowers.

They droop like I've pounded them with a rug beater, and I come to my senses. I can hear Mama Lu. "Rinse water on the flowers. Soapy water to scrub the porch." I try to clear the soap off the flowers with clear rinse water, but the marigolds don't seem to notice my help.

By the time Edwin comes home for supper, I've fed Mama Lu's chickens and her cats, finished the wash, rinsed the flowers twice over, and made supper. When I tell my brother about Emory's mishap, he smiles.

"You did just right for a jelly sting. Mama Lu and Pa would be mighty proud."

I go to bed that night wondering about my mother. If she'd stayed, would she have shown me how to make cactus jelly or cobbler? How to wash clothes? What to do with the used-up water? I doubt she would know how to treat the hard knock of a jellyfish sting.

But she might have taught me the ways of being beautiful.

SEVENTEEN

traipse—*to walk*

Early the next morning, I **traipse** back to the Lavenders' place and return their jug and vinegar. I knock loud on their door, but no one stirs inside. With a heap of relief, I set the jug by the door and tear out. The best way to meet up with Hortense and Aurelia Lavender is not at all.

As I turn toward the ocean, I see Pa and his crew hauling the surfboat into the water for the Tuesday drill. They'll row fast and hard out beyond the shoals. Sometimes the Keeper deliberately capsizes the boat to give the crew practice turning it right side up.

Clouds hang overhead when I feed Mama Lu's chickens and gather eggs. Rain hangs in the air like it's trying to decide whether to drop on our island or move on.

It might just as well stay here. There's no sign of Will or Emory. Though I'm usually disinclined to do so, I start cleaning the house. Our cottage is not large. All one floor. A big room for cooking, eating, and sitting. The men part of my family share a sleeping room, and I have a curtained cubby that Pa added off the kitchen. Dusting goes fast. I sweep up and use a bucket of yesterday's wash water to scrub the floors.

The rain's moved on by afternoon, but still no Will or Emory. I don't need them for entertainment. I can cook up some on my own. 'Sides, what I have in mind wouldn't please Will a bit. I'm going to build me a lookout tower like Pa has at the station. I surely won't get help from a pesky boy reminding me that I can't ever be a Life-Saver.

Mortimer and Mildred wait for me on Mama Lu's porch when I go to her woodpile. They swirl their tails in greeting and settle back to their layabout ways.

Everyone on Whisper Island keeps lumber odds and ends for just-in-case building. Most comes from shipwrecks or buildings that bad storms have blown down. Edwin's used all ours making a porch bench for Katrina's granny, so I borrow a few boards from Mama Lu.

Four short planks will make perfect ladder steps. Next thing—find a sturdy piece for the floor. A wide, flat board is wedged in tight between two heavy timbers.

After some tugging, I pull it loose so suddenly that I sit down hard on the ground. And come face to face with a snake. He seems as surprised as I am. We disappear in opposite directions. He slithers back under the pile, and I drag my boards to the path.

Will sorely dislikes snakes. Good thing he isn't here, although watching him throw a fit would be agreeable!

After a sweaty hour nailing my ladder steps to an oak, I realize I need help hefting up boards to build a platform. I could use those two boys. I decide to pay Emory a call. Reverend Sewell says it's our Christian duty to visit the sick and infirm. I guess being jelly stung makes the grade of being infirm.

When I open the Sperry gate, Aunt Marcelle bustles over from her garden. "Hey, Primmy. Too soon for weed pulling. I'll let you know when I need your help."

"I came to look in on Emory." I smile, but she answers with a frown.

"Emory's not fit to be looked in on. Not fit to be looked *at*. That boy's somehow added poison ivy to his miseries." She shakes her head so hard her sunbonnet slips off. "He can get into more mischief and trouble than any one soul. He'll be out of sight for a few days while I dose him."

I long to view Emory for myself, but I have to take his aunt's word that he's not fit to be seen.

I think of stopping at Miz Crocker's. She might still have some of my sweet potato cobbler. I second-think myself. Hoping to get some of your own apology food doesn't seem right, although it would be a mighty good treat.

I've about reached our cottage when I hear Will calling.

"Hey, Primmy."

I turn and see him just ahead of Mama Lu. They're loaded down with packages. I meet them at Mama Lu's gate and swing it open.

"Thank you, Primmy." Mama Lu leans on her walking stick and hands me her bundles.

Will's face has disappeared behind two big boxes, one squarish, one round.

"I missed you." This remark is meant for Mama Lu, but Will takes it for himself.

"I been busy," he says. "Helping Pa mend the roof."

"Good thing to do with storm season coming on," Mama Lu tells him. "How long's your pa home for?"

"He ships out tomorrow." Will's father is a sea captain and sometimes is gone for months. Except for his baby sister, Will and his ma are alone most of the time.

"Will, put these parcels in the house," Mama Lu says. "Then you'd best get home for supper."

Will does as he's told. "So long." He waves and takes off down the path.

"Thank you for looking after things whilst I was gone, Primmy," Mama Lu says.

"You're welcome. Why don't you have supper with Edwin and me?"

She shakes her head. "'Fraid not. I'm plumb tuckered out. I'll see you tomorrow."

She closes her door and leaves me standing on the porch, still wondering what business she had in Cranston.

At supper Edwin reminds me of my weeding job for Reverend Sewell. "Today's rain should make weeding easy tomorrow."

As if *anything* could make weeding easy!

EIGHTEEN

cockamamie—*strange, peculiar*

Wednesday morning, I muck out Pansy's sty and stop my chores to rest a bit in Pa's rocker.

Will pushes the door open and comes right in. "Morning, Primmy. Got any harebrained plans for today?"

"I'm building a lookout tower and could use your help." It pains me to admit this, but it's the truth.

"A lookout tower!" His scowl shows his poor opinion as he picks my apron off its hook. "You'd best spend your time learning to cook and sew."

"I'll spend my time as I please." I stomp outside to the tree where I dumped my load of wood. I pull a hammer from the loop on my overalls and reach in a pocket for nails. Will stands by, laughing, as I pound them into the ladder steps I started the day before. The third nail bends sideways, and I bang the hammer onto my thumb.

Questionable language escapes out of me, and I blink back tears.

"You all right?" Will stops laughing and tries to pat my shoulder. I push him away.

"Leave me be!" I take out for the house and slam the door behind me.

Presently, Will comes in with a pail of water. He pours some in a mug, plunks my hand into the pail, and hands me the mug. "Here. This'll help. Drink it slow."

Instead, I take big gulps. The throbbing eases, as do my tears. I stop my questionable language as well. I hope Reverend Sewell hasn't heard.

We sit a spell without a word passing between us. Then Will clears his throat. I notice he's still pressing my hand down in the water. "Seems like one of us takes over when the other is flummoxed, Primmy. You knew right quick what to do for Emory's jelly sting, and I knew cold water would help your sore thumb. We're a good match."

What? Where did he come up with such a **cockamamie** *notion?*

I sit up straight. Snatch my hand from under his.

Shake it hard. Walk to the doorway. Fumble with the latch.

Change the subject!

"Uh, it was mighty nice of you to carry Mama Lu's packages for her." The words squeak out of me.

"Glad to," he mumbles and looks at the table.

"Seems like she came back with a lot of goods. I've never known her to need that much of anything."

Will sits like a rock, not offering any information.

I sigh. "Any idea what she bought?"

He shakes his head. "Nope. Some parcels were soft. Couldn't tell what was in the boxes 'cause they was all wrapped up."

No help at all.

Will advises against further lookout building because of my smashed thumb.

For a change, I agree with him. He stays on to share thick slices of bread and goat cheese.

"I reckon I'll stop in to see how Emory's doing," Will says. "Ma heard he's got poison ivy bad. Wanna come?'

"Nope. I'm due to weed the church cemetery."

We part company, and I head to the ocean side of our island. From the path leading to church, I can see Pa and his crew practicing with the signal flags. Jacob is waving the big red flag that stands for the Morse code *dash*, and Emory's pa holds the white flag for *dot*. I prefer the colorful banners, one for each letter of the alphabet. They're all right pretty, but my favorite is a blue-and-white checkerboard that means *N*, as in *NO*.

After watching for a few minutes, I mosey on and knock at Reverend Sewell's door. His wife—a short, thin woman—answers. She smiles as if I'm making a social call. "Why, hello, Primmy. Have you come to do the weeds?"

"Yes, ma'am."

"I didn't know if you'd come this week, what with your trip across the Sound and all."

One thing about Whisper Island—everyone knows your plans almost before you do.

"After you finish, dear, come in for a glass of lemonade."

I thank her, hoping she won't want to talk about my trip.

The graveyard isn't big. Leastways it doesn't look big with all the weeds crowded inside the weathered fence. I've never had occasion to visit here, seeing as how no kin of mine are buried yet. Pa brings flowers to his first wife's grave on her birthday, but I've never come along.

I decide to start in one corner, work my way around the edges, and then go for the middle. I've pulled a passel of old thistles and mullein when my knuckle hits a rough spot. I've run up against a headstone. I clear away the clover tangle at its base and make out the name: *Gerda Bachmeier*. Herr Bachmeier's wife! A little bunch of wildflowers is stuck between the fence slats behind the marker. I bend over to read the rest of the words:

GERDA BACHMEIER

1850 – 1898

Ein Engel

A carved-out figure of an angel tells me what the German words mean. I sit back on my heels and ponder what it would be like to die some place where folks talked in a language different from your own. Worse yet, to live with strange words all around you.

Little Ginny Pratt's gravestone is free of weeds and looks like her ma just scrubbed it.

GINNY PRATT

1907 – 1912

Sweet flower fair from us now gone
We'll meet you soon in heaven's dawn.

I remember that dear little girl and how she loved to go treasure hunting. Then it strikes me: when I die, my mother won't be here to look after my grave.

As I move on, I try to pull this thought away with each weed I yank up. It hangs on like a dandelion root.

·Cattycorner from Mrs. Bachmeier's plot, I neaten the grave of Pa's first wife, Alice:

ALICE HOPKINS

1870 – 1897

Beloved wife
Tender mother
Faithful friend
Mourned by all who knew her

More anger knots my insides. Why couldn't my mother have been like Alice? Rose Alene Whitney Hopkins seems to care nothing about being a beloved wife or tender mother. From what I can fathom, she can't even bother herself to be a faithful friend.

Fury eats at me as I finish my chore, tugging at every ugly weed I find. I end with scraped knuckles and raw feelings.

Even Mrs. Sewell's sweet company and cold lemonade can't smooth them away, and I'm grateful she doesn't ask about my trip to Cranston.

NINETEEN

Persian Pickle—*droplet-shaped design originating in India, sometimes called paisley*

After I spend a restless night filled with worries, sunshine greets me on Thursday. Later, when I put bread to rise, I notice the wall calendar next to the stove. August 14, just four days from my birthday. Four days until my trip across the Sound. This makes me itchy, like my skin is ready to jump away and start for the mailboat without me.

I've no idea how to ready myself for this trip, unsure what to take along. I examine the hooks in my little cubby. My only passable shirtwaist is about to pop its seams, but it'll have to do. My worn brown skirt looks sad. An extra pair of drawers hangs with my petticoat. Both need mending, and the petticoat is so dingy it's gray. I spread my clothes on the bed. Not much to pack. Then I realize I left my shoes at the station when I visited Pa.

Will my beautiful mother want to spend time with a barefoot girl dressed in tatters?

I'd thought Mama Lu would help me plan this trip. But since she's came back from Cranston, she seems too busy to do more than say "howdy."

I look around our little cottage and try to imagine what it might be like to stay at a hotel. Will I have a place of my own for sleeping? Sometimes I've thought I'd like to fly off this island, but now I feel like a baby bird about to fledge from its safe nest. My mother will be the only one around if I fall. So far in my life, she's been no help to me in any which way.

To take my mind off what's to come, I pick up my hammer and nails to work on the lookout tower. When I get to Pansy's pen, I stop and shake my fist at her. "I wish Pa would go with me. Or Mama Lu."

Pansy grunts, as if to say, "Your ma didn't invite anyone else." She trots away to chew on some food scraps she's left uneaten.

I sigh and look at the stepping boards I pounded into the tree yesterday. Might as well give up my lookout plans. I can't build a tower by myself, and Will's dead set against helping with anything that reminds him I want to be a Life-Saver.

Next I go to fetch sweet potatoes from the root bin, but it's empty. Now what? I promised Emory I'd save him some cobbler from tonight's supper. It would be a special treat, what with all the miseries he's come by.

I'll borrow some potatoes from Mama Lu.

She's at the table, cutting away with her sewing shears. Shiny blue cloth falls away as she trims it to the shape of a tissue pattern.

"Morning, Mama Lu." I lean close to see what her cutting will produce.

"Morning, Primmy." She keeps at her work, not looking up.

"I came to borrow some sweet potatoes."

"Help yourself. You know where they are." She doesn't stop her cutting.

Cut-out pieces of blue and green **Persian Pickle** cotton are neatly stacked on her sewing machine. The pieces hide the painted flowers on the machine's surface. When I was little I sat on Mama Lu's lap and traced the roses while she sewed. I bobbed up and down as she worked the treadle.

"Making yourself some dresses?"

"Nope. Not for me." She keeps working those shears.

"Mighty pretty colors."

"I like 'em right fine myself." She finally looks up.

"You'd best get those taters. Borrow one of my baskets. Hurry on now. The day'll get away from you afore you know it."

Prickly at being sent away, I fill a basket and slam the door behind me.

I'm rolling out biscuit dough when Will comes along, pulling his little sister Rowena in a wagon. Her sunbonnet's so big I can barely see her face, but I know she's got the same flaming hair as her brother.

I go out to greet them. "Hey there, Wena." I bend down to tickle her fat little belly.

Will looks hard at me. "Ma told me last night that you're going over to Cranston to see your ma. How come you never told me?"

"I only just decided." *A week ago.* "Anyways, I didn't see any need for you to know," I mumble. "I figured you'd laugh or tell me it's a bad idea."

"Why would I laugh? It seems mighty important to see your ma after all this time. Is your pa going too?'

"No, her letter invited just me."

"When're you going?"

"Monday." I could do without his questions!

"But that's your birthday," he mutters. "I thought—"

"You thought *what*?"

"N-nothing." He fidgets with his shirttail.

Rowena starts fussing just then, and Will bends to

comfort her. "I'd best get home so's Ma can feed her. See you tomorrow, Primmy."

He disappears down the path.

A few minutes later, I'm on my way to return Mama Lu's basket when I see someone stepping off her porch. My mouth drops open.

It's Elspeth Thornton, and she's looking mighty pleased. Like maybe she knows someone's making her a dress out of shiny blue goods.

I spend the rest of the afternoon in a huff. It's too hot to stay inside, so I settle in the tree stump chair with *Alice's Adventures in Wonderland*. Mama Lu passed that book on to me when I turned ten. Alice's story sounds like mine. Nothing is the way it should be.

Mama Lu is most likely making new dresses for Elspeth Thornton. Pa and Jacob are living at the station. Edwin's good enough company, but his mind is mostly on Katrina and how to please her. Emory's so covered with miseries that he's not fit for adventuring. And Will's turned up with strange ideas about him and me.

I sigh and close the book. Pansy trots over to grunt at me from her pen.

"You're lucky," I tell her. "No one expects anything from you. All you have to do is be a sow. Have a litter now and again. Eat and sleep and roll around in the dirt.

You probably don't know your ma either, but that doesn't bother you one bit."

I tuck the book under my arm and go inside. Might as well start supper. Edwin promised some ocean trout to fry up. After roast corn and sliced tomatoes, supper will end with my cobbler. A fine meal for a lonely widower.

TWENTY

meehonkey—*old-time name for hide-and-seek*

When Herr Bachmeier arrives, Edwin sits on the porch with him while I fry fish and drop corn in boiling water. A short time later, we're at the table, digging into our food.

"Primmy's crossing the Sound next week." Edwin talks over our guest's eating noise.

"Yah," Herr Bachmeier replies. "To see her mother. And this is something you want to do, *Klöbchen?*"

I nod.

"That's not all," my brother says. "Primmy wants to be a surfman like Pa and Jacob."

Why does he keep bringing that up?

"Crossing the Sound in that ol' mailboat might

change her mind. She'll get a good idea how hard working on water can be."

Herr Bachmeier nods but says nothing.

"We try to tell her that she can't never join the Life-Saving Service on account of bein' a girl, but she won't listen."

"But things change," Herr Bachmeier says. "Life brings many surprises. Some good. Some hard. People now can fly in the air and ride in automobiles."

Edwin frowns. "Bunch of crazy notions, to my way of thinking. Anyways, a girl should stay home and take care of her family."

The two men go on and on. I say nothing. This conversation always ends at the same place: I'm a girl. Girls can't be Life-Savers. Ever.

As he takes a second helping of cobbler, Herr Bachmeier smiles at me. "Perhaps there are other ways you can help when a ship wrecks."

"Don't go puttin' ideas in her head!"

"Ah! I think Primmy's head already holds many good ideas."

Shaking his own noggin hard, Edwin excuses himself and takes off to "help Nate."

"And now I must go, *Klöbchen*." Herr Bachmeier pushes his chair back from the table. "A most wonderful meal. *Danke*."

"Wait!" I follow him to the door. "Do you think I'm right to meet my mother?"

"Yah. I believe you wonder about her. This trip will answer your questions."

"Did you ever meet her?" I've asked more about my mother in the last week than I have for the whole of my life.

"Yah. I know her since she was a beautiful baby. My Gerda and I were her godparents."

He's known my mother her whole life! My throat closes and I swallow hard. "Does she write to you?"

His smile disappears. "Nein. Godparents are forgotten as children grow old."

My mother abandoned him too.

Friday's air is hot and thick. The walk to Emory's house feels like pushing through boiled pudding.

When I get to the Sperry place, no one's in sight. "Emory? Miz Hoover?" No answer, so I leave the cobbler on the kitchen table. I consider going to the station, but I know the crew is busy practicing ways to revive folks who appear to have drowned. Then Pa'll give instructions for bandaging and taking care of survivors. He'll have no time for me, so I plod back home.

The day drags by, as if the heat has slowed it. I spend more time fretting about my trip. Pa's sent word to the hotel that I'd be coming to Cranston on the mailboat. I wish he hadn't. Then my mother wouldn't know for sure that I've accepted her invitation. I could just stay here with my old clothes and bare feet.

I'm wondering what I'll cook for Edwin's meal when I hear Mama Lu calling from the path.

She's come to ask me for supper. "Your pa and Jacob have a shift off, so they'll be there. If Edwin can spare a few hours away from Katrina, he might be with us as well. We'll have us a right proper family supper."

Why is she being so friendly and nice after barely speaking to me all week? I don't ask, for fear her answer will be: "Because I've been busy sewing new dresses for Elspeth."

Instead, I accept her invitation.

Pa and Jacob wait on Mama Lu's porch. I wonder if they've brought my shoes. We go inside, and I see that Mama Lu's put away all her sewing goods. I start to take my place at the table, but the others move to the parlor.

"Come here, Primmy," Pa says. "I want to talk to you."

My heart jumps. I try to think what I've done wrong

since I last saw him. Nothing that he would know about.
I sit down beside him.

"Close your eyes," Mama Lu commands, as if we're
about to play **meehonkey**.

Puzzled, I close my eyes and listen to whispers and
rustlings and feet shuffling around me.

"Open 'em up!" Jacob says.

My brothers hold up two dresses. Jacob's is shiny
blue and Edwin has the Persian Pickle. A straw bonnet
with flowers and a blue ribbon teeters on Pa's head. He
hands it to me with a pair of black leather shoes. Mama
Lu spreads out a new petticoat and a white shirtwaist.
She leans toward me.

"I have new drawers for you as well," she whispers.

"Try one, Primmy," Jacob says. "Let's see how it
looks on you."

My face burns and I shake my head. What if it's too
snug? My brothers will howl.

"You men go out on the porch whilst Primmy
changes," Mama Lu orders.

A few minutes later, I'm dressed in shiny blue. It
seems a right good fit, and I run to the scrap of mirror
Mama Lu keeps above her washbasin. I can only see
myself a glimpse at a time. I hope there's a big looking-
glass somewhere in Cranston.

Mama Lu claps her hands. "You look like a proper

lady, Primmy." She calls the men to come inside.

My brothers stare at me like they've never seen me before. They've surely never seen *this* me before!

Pa grins big and gives me a hug. "Happy birthday, Primmy. You'll go across the Sound in grand style."

I can't think what to say. I just grin right back and know that everyone here in this little cottage loves me.

TWENTY-ONE

say a word—*talk a lot*

Saturday is a whirl of activity. I spend most of it with Mama Lu. She lends me her red carpetbag for my trip and shows me how to fold my clothes so that they won't turn into a mess of wrinkles.

She's added some finery to my blue dress. "Miz Thornton sent this scrap of lace to go around the collar. Makes it right fancy."

"Elspeth's ma?" I ask.

"Yep. Elspeth brought it around yesterday, but I didn't have time to sew it on."

"When I saw her coming out of your house with a big smile, I thought you were making those dresses for her."

"Land, child, why would I do that? Her ma orders everything from the Sears catalog."

"But why was she smiling?" I couldn't picture Elspeth Thornton being happy about doing me a favor.

"I told her next time Mildred birthed a litter, I'd give her a kitten."

Oh.

Sunday afternoon, Will and I visit Emory. His poison ivy spots have faded to a dull pink.

He grins when he sees us at the door. "Auntie won't let me out of her sight. Took me to a Ladies Guild meetin' on Friday. Those ladies sure can **say a word** whilst they sew! I'm tired of being cooped up. Auntie says I can get myself in trouble just walking the lane."

Will pokes me with his elbow. "Sounds like *you.*"

I pretend not to hear.

Emory sighs. "I sure envy you goin' across the Sound."

"I'll be back before you know it. Now I'd best get home." I head for the path. Will's right behind me.

"Mind if I walk along?" he asks.

"Makes me no never mind," I mumble.

We're near my cottage when Will stops. "Hold on a minute."

Now what?

He stares at me. Fiddles with his shirttail. Clears his throat.

"I'm in a hurry." I put my hand on our gate.

"Wait!" He pushes his hand in a pocket and pulls out a sparkly blue stone on a gold chain. "Here. For your birthday."

I stare at my gift.

"Well, ain't you gonna take it?" His voice squeaks. "I found it last spring and been polishing it up as best I could."

"Thank you." My hand shakes. "It's right pretty."

"Happy birthday." He punches my shoulder and runs off.

Boys are a head-scratching puzzle. First they're nice. Then they hit you.

I go inside and busy myself with packing. Before I go to bed, I pull my mother's picture from my Bible. "I'll see you in person tomorrow. I hope you'll be purely nice to me, with no surprise knocks." I tuck the picture and Will's chain into the pocket of my new blue dress.

I'm awake long before Edwin calls me. "Happy Birthday, Primmy. If you're gonna catch the mailboat, you'd best get out of bed."

I button up the new shirtwaist and pull on my brown

skirt. Mama Lu thought it best to save my fancy dresses for the Virginia Dare Hotel.

When I step onto the porch, blustery wind and thick, dark clouds greet me. My stomach knots. Crossing the Sound in a hard blow is bound to be unpleasant.

"Gonna be a rough trip, Primmy. We'd best get you there early enough to find space under the canvas cover. Sitting aft in a storm helps." He hands me a thick slice of bread. "Eat it on the way to the boat." He takes my slicker off its hook. "You'll need this."

I frown. My old oilskin is not a good match for my fancy dresses, but it's protection from the stormy weather that's coming. I cram my new hat into the carpetbag.

As we hurry down the path, rain pelts us hard.

"Pa won't come to say good-bye," I mutter as we near the dock. "On account of the weather."

"He'll be sore disappointed," Edwin answers. "He intended to see you off."

I reach over to squeeze my brother's hand. He stretches his arm around my shoulders and hugs me close. "You'll be fine, Primmy. Remember that we're all waiting for you to come back."

Homer Clackhunt waits at the top of the mailboat ramp. "'Morning, Primmy. Edwin. Gonna be a rough crossing. But we'll get you there, young lady. Come aboard." He takes my carpetbag from Edwin.

I turn to give my brother a hug. "Tell Pa and Jacob good-bye."

He nods. "See you on Wednesday."

When I step onto the boat, I feel it lurch in the choppy water. I hurry out of the rain and sit on a bench under the canvas roof. Miz Crocker's oldest granddaughter, Martha, looks up and smiles. "Hey, Primmy. Looks like we're in for a rough ride this morning. I'm on my way to meet my cousin Arletta. I hear you're going to see your ma."

I nod.

Soon the benches fill with people. Some islanders. Some strangers: Martin Forrest leads two sheep onto the open deck. He goes back for a crate of chickens and a case of tomatoes.

Martha leans toward me. "For the big birthday celebration at the Virginia Dare Hotel."

Birthday celebration? My mother hasn't forgotten my birthday, after all. She's ordered a surprise celebration at the hotel! I smile at the thought of being the guest of honor.

Martha goes on. "It's Virginia Dare's birthday. The hotel always does it up big."

Oh.

The gray gloom overhead matches my dark mood. I'm about to stand and run back down the ramp, but it's too late. My anger grows as Homer Clackhunt moves the boat away from the dock.

TWENTY-TWO

quamished—*sick to the stomach*

The wind lets loose when we pull into the Sound. It hits full force, pitching the boat so high that I reel hard to the left. Suddenly the boat drops low, and I'm joggled off the seat. I grip the edge of the bench and dig in my heels to keep from hitting the floor. Each bump and jolt sends my stomach in the opposite direction, and I'm glad I had a meager breakfast.

Pa gave me some advice to avoid being seasick: "Imagine you're riding the waves. Sit up straight as you're able and move with the boat. Keep your eyes on the horizon if you can." I try this and it helps some, but my stomach is still unsettled.

"Ohhh." Martha clutches my arm with a cold, damp hand. Her face is pale, and she shivers. "Primmy, help me." She bends over, gripping her middle. She's **qua-mished** for sure, and I fight to keep my own stomach quiet.

I remember Edwin's words to Herr Bachmeier: "Crossing the Sound in that ol' mailboat might change her mind. She'll get a good idea how hard working on water can be."

Here's my chance to prove him wrong. I pull off my slicker and hand it to Martha. "This will warm you some."

She struggles into the coat and squeezes my hands so hard I fear they'll lose feeling.

"Now stay close to me and hold yourself straight." I work to keep my voice steady.

Together we try to move with the chopping waves. I pray that the wind will let up. Instead, it grows worse. Waves slap the sides of the boat and slosh onto the deck. The sheep loudly complain from the foredeck, and the chickens put up a fuss. Icy rain splashes in under the canvas and drenches us. Martha's teeth chatter. I can feel her tremble through the slicker.

Suddenly she turns to me and looks about to say something. Instead, her breakfast erupts onto my skirt.

I gag and try to push down the bitter taste rising in my throat. My stomach churns. I breathe deep, only to draw in the sour smell. I swallow hard.

Martha sobs. "Oh, Primmy, I'm so sorry. Ma warned me not to eat a big breakfast, but I was so hungry and—"

I clench my fists, determined to keep from losing my own breakfast. "Turn around so you can see the water. It might help to see the waves coming."

She does as I say and calms somewhat. I take stock of the damage. My skirt is ruined. The rain has turned my hair to pure fuzz, like dandelion seed fluff. My clothes and shoes are soaked. I'm grateful that Homer put my carpetbag in the cabin below deck. At least my new clothes will be dry.

I huddle on the bench with Martha and wonder how much longer this wretched trip will last. I'm sorry that I agreed to cross the Sound.

By the time we arrive at Cranston, the storm has eased and Martha seems to be over her discomfort. As soon as Homer lowers the ramp onto the dock, she pushes past other passengers to get off the boat first. "'Bye, Primmy. Have a nice visit!" She waves and hurries to hug her cousin.

She's taken my slicker. I'm left with a sour skirt and no way to cover it. As I wait for Homer to bring my carpetbag, I'm surprised to see Herr Bachmeier step out from the cabin. I smile and walk toward him.

"Guten Tag, Herr Bachmeier."

"Guten Tag, Klöbchen."

"Are you going to see my mother?"

He shakes his head. *"Nein."* He tips his hat and hurries away.

I stare after him. Why has he crossed the Sound? Mama Lu says he's never set foot off our island since his wife died.

"Here, little lady." Homer hands me the carpetbag. "Time to meet your ma." He frowns at my skirt. "Mayhap we should rinse you off first."

My face burns with embarrassment. I'm not fit to be seen—or sniffed.

Homer brings out a brush and a bucket of soapy water. While he helps Martin Forrest unload the animals, I scrub Martha's breakfast away. No amount of rubbing gets rid of the stink.

Homer comes back for me and looks at my skirt. "That's better. No one'll ever know there was a mess."

I don't share his opinion, but I pick up my carpetbag and follow him onto the dock. My steps wobble, and the pavement seems to roll under my feet.

Homer chuckles. "You're still on your sea legs. Just take it easy 'til you get your land legs back."

I steady myself on a post and look around. No beautiful woman. Did she see me and leave in disgust?

"We landed a mite early," Homer says. "Your ma'll be along in a minute or two. Just sit down."

Hunched on a crate, I hug Mama Lu's carpetbag to my chest and rest my head on the soft bag.

"Miss Primrose Hopkins! Miss Primrose Hopkins!"

A tall, thin man stands a few feet away. In spite of the steamy day, he wears a brown suit and black tie. He turns this way and that as he searches the dock. When he comes to me, he frowns.

Homer steps up just then. "Mr. Grayson. How are you, sir? You've come for Primmy, I see."

Mr. Grayson and I stare at each other. He seems unhappy with the state of things. I feel the same.

He snatches up my bag and stalks away.

"Follow me."

TWENTY-THREE

ragamuffin—*shabbily clothed, dirty child*

Homer pats my shoulder. "It's all right, Primmy. Mr. Grayson works at the hotel. I reckon your ma sent him to tote your bag."

Unhappy with how my visit has started, I struggle to keep up with Mr. Grayson. He moves quickly around the corner, away from the dock. We turn onto a brick-paved street and step up on the wooden sidewalk. Stores mix in with two-story houses like Elspeth Thornton's. An automobile chugs past, and I marvel how it moves along without a horse pulling it.

A few folks stroll past and stare at me. I take care to keep my eyes cast downward and see that everyone, even the children, wears shoes. In August!

The grandest building I've ever seen stands at the

end of the road. Green shutters and baskets of red flowers prettify the white walls. The sign above the long porch reads: VIRGINIA DARE HOTEL. I stop to take in all this fanciness.

"Come along!" Mr. Grayson barks over his shoulder. "I've no time to lollygag."

"Yessir." His highfalutin bossiness makes me wish his long legs would tangle and land him in the dirty water pooling at the street edges.

Finally, we're walking up the steps to the hotel porch. On either side of the grand front door, palm trees grow in pots big enough that I could climb in one and hide from Will.

My mouth drops open when we step inside. The big hall would suit a queen's palace. My new shoes click against the marble floor. To my right, an unhappy-looking man stands behind a counter. An open cabinet of little shelves hangs on the wall behind him. Across the hall, a sign tells me there's a dining room beyond the double doors. A grand marble staircase rises directly ahead and curves down to end in two posts. A naked lady statue stands on one post, and a lion statue rests on the other.

The sour-looking man leans over the counter toward Mr. Grayson. "*That's* her daughter?" he mutters. "That **ragamuffin**?"

I stiffen and twist my hands into my soiled skirt. My face burns. I stare at the marble floor.

"Yes. Send Titus up to tell her."

The man rings a little bell. A boy not much bigger than me comes running. He stops just long enough to hear his instructions and runs off again.

Mr. Grayson points at a wooden bench by the counter. "Sit there." He drops my carpetbag at my feet, struts across the hall, and disappears through the dining room doors.

I try to smooth my skirt. The new shirtwaist is wrinkled beyond help, and I wonder at the state of things inside the red carpetbag. I wait for my mother to rescue me from the mean spirit of the man behind the counter.

"Where is she? Primrose?"

A thin woman grips the railing as she trundles down the stairs. Her long purple dress balloons out from an embroidered satin belt at her waist to a band just below her knees. This leg belt is so tight that she can hardly move from one step to the next. Her hair is wrapped up in some sparkly fabric with two bright green feathers waving out at the back.

My heart pounds. Is this the woman whose picture is in my Bible?

She nearly trips on the last step but clutches the naked lady's ankle to keep her balance. She shuffles toward the counter. A syrupy scent fills the air as she passes by. I shrink into myself, frozen to the bench. I wish with all my heart to be back home.

She looks around the hall and turns to the sour-looking man. "Titus said my daughter was here. Where is she?"

He points at me.

The sound of her heavy sigh fills the hall.

I duck my head and pray that she'll go back to her room and leave me in peace. There's still time to board Homer's boat and go back to Whisper Island.

Her shoes clatter across the marble floor, and she stands over me. "Primrose Estella?"

"Yes, ma'am." I look up, hoping to see her smile.

She pats my shoulder. "You poor thing! Come with me."

I snatch up Mama Lu's carpetbag and go with her. We move slowly because of her leg belt. When we reach the top of the stairs, we turn right and stop in front of the door marked *213*.

She turns a key in the lock, pushes the door open, and pulls me inside.

Before I can say anything, she walks across the room and opens another door. "This is the bathroom. I'm sure you'd like a nice hot bath. Then I have a surprise for you."

A large white tub with handles marked *Hot* and *Cold*

sits on metal legs that look like lion paws. Nothing like my Saturday night bath in Mama Lu's kitchen. I look from my mother to the tub and back again.

She must remember that we have no such tubs on Whisper Island because she moves past me and twists the handles. Water gushes out. "My favorite soap is in that little dish, and here are some nice, fluffy towels. You'll feel better after you bathe."

For sure I'll look and smell better!

Next she shows me how to pull the chain to empty the commode. When she finally closes the door, I set the carpetbag on a little stool under the window. I use the commode, take off my ruined clothes, and slide into the hot water. Soon every inch of me, hair to toes, is wet. The soap smells like lilies of the valley. It brings a memory:

Someone hands me a flower. "See the little white bells, Primrose? Aren't they pretty?"

The soap slips from my hand, and the memory is gone.

Later, I step out of the bathroom in my undervest and drawers. My mother waits with the surprise she promised.

TWENTY-FOUR

flibbertigibbet—*a flighty person*

She flutters a pink dress that looks like the icing on Elspeth Thornton's fancy birthday cake. "I bought this special for you, Primrose, for Virginia Dare's birthday supper. We'll turn every head in the dining room!"

If heads turn in my direction, they'll laugh when they see this get-up. My mother's a **flibbertigibbet** to buy a dress for someone she hasn't seen in nine years. Plus, it's nonsensical to celebrate the birthday of someone who died centuries ago. Especially when you're standing right smack in front of a live person whose birthday you forgot.

"I can hardly wait to see how lovely you look."

She has more faith in my ability to look lovely than I

do. I want nothing to do with this silly dress, but I raise my arms and stand like a stone while she drops it over my head. The skirt goes past my shoulders and arms, then stops, stuck on my dumpling belly. With tugging on her part and grunting on mine, we finally squeeze the dress over my middle. I feel like a pink sausage. The neckline dips below the top of my vest, and the sleeves hang off my shoulders. The long skirt puddles around my feet. I don't need a mirror to know that I look ridiculous.

"I thought you'd be taller by now," my mother complains.

It's not my fault that I'm too short for her "surprise." I'm also too plump and flat-chested.

"I have two new dresses," I say. "I'll wear one to this fancy party."

"What store did they come from?"

"Mama Lu made them for me. For my birthday, *which is today.*"

She doesn't seem to hear that last part. "Mama Lu? How is she?"

Before I can answer, she's peeling the dress back up and over my head. "Let me see those homemade frocks. Maybe I can do something with them." She tosses the pink dress onto an armchair.

I open the carpetbag and shake out my two dresses. They're wrinkled. My new hat is squashed, but the

petticoat shakes out crisp and bright. I spread everything on the bed. My stomach clenches as I wait for her
judgment.

She ignores the clothes and rummages through my
belongings. "Where are your gloves?" She holds up my
stockings. "Too dark!" She pokes and pulls. "No summer
slippers? Those black things will never do."

I cross my arms tight around my middle. "They're
brand new. Pa gave them to me for my birthday, *which
is today.*"

She sniffs. "Just like a man to choose something dark
and dreary for his daughter's birth—your birthday? Did
I miss it?"

You've missed it for nine years. My fists tighten. I look
outside. Tips of red geraniums poke up from the window
box. "It's today."

"Oh, that's right! Your father wanted to name you
Virginia Dare because you were born on her birthday."
She flits around the room like a butterfly trying to decide
which flower to light on. Suddenly she twirls around to
face me. "Let's go shopping!"

With a sigh, I stand up.

She changes her mind quicker than an eyeblink.
"Better yet, I'll go pick out some pretty things for you.
Wait here. You'll have the best birthday ever!"

She sweeps out the door.

I move to the big, soft bed and lie on my back, next to my new dresses. Tears well up and roll down my cheeks. This day has taken the starch right out of me.

"Primrose Estella! Wake up! Look what I've found."

I scoot up to sit against the pillows. The wall clock tells me it's past five o'clock.

She drops several packages on the bed. "Open them. They're all for you." She sits in the armchair and claps her hands like a little child waiting for a treat.

I feel older than my mother as she watches me. Each brown paper package holds something white. Lace gloves. Silk stockings. Shoes with a strap across the top of my foot. A lace-trimmed camisole to replace my undervest.

I should probably make a big to-do. All I can muster is, "Thank you."

"There's one more very special gift that's being delivered." She lights the lamp on the bedside table. "Now it's time to get dressed, Primrose."

While my mother bathes, I put on my new finery. I don't feel like Primmy Hopkins until I button up my blue dress. A long mirror on the wall opposite the bed lets me see all of myself at once. I add Will's gold chain and admire the person looking back at me. I turn this way and that. My skirt twirls out around me. I can hardly believe how fine I look! Not like a dumpling at all.

My mother steps out of the bathroom in a green silk dress that floats from a golden satin band belted above her waist. Her head wrap is the same satin, and narrow satin straps hold the dress on her shoulders. Rose Alene Whitney Hopkins is beautiful. A beautiful **flibbertigibbet**.

I wait for her praise as she looks me over.

Instead, she sighs. "Let's pretty up your hair!"

I washed my hair good in the bathtub and brushed it out as best I could. What was she going to do to it? I back away and shake my head.

She pays no mind and rummages through a leather case. "I have just the thing to keep it in place."

As she walks toward me with two sparkly clips, another memory comes:

Someone shows me a shiny pink ribbon. "For my pretty girl's hair."

She yanks my frizz tight behind my ears and pokes the clips in place. The memory is gone.

"There!" She points to the mirror. "Isn't that better?'

My head looks like a peeled apple. I'm about to tell her that it's worse, not better, when my hair escapes from the clips and straggles back over my ears.

"Oh, for heaven's sakes." She tosses the clips away

and pulls out one of her head wraps. At least it's blue to match my dress, but it's too fussy to match *me*. She pulls it across my forehead and ties it to one side. I look like a foolish pirate.

"Perfect!" she coos.

TWENTY-FIVE

reticule—*small drawstring handbag*

A knock at the door interrupts her fussing. She opens it a crack. "Thank you, Titus."

She hands me a box wrapped in silver-and-gold paper. "Now for your special birthday present. Open it!" She claps her hands again.

It's a small drawstring bag like the one Mama Lu uses to keep her dried seeds. Mama Lu's is plain muslin, but this one is peacock-blue satin and lace with beaded fringe. "Thank you," I mumble. "It's a real nice bag."

"Silly! It's not just a *bag*. It's a **reticule**, and I had your initials embroidered on the inside."

Sure enough, *PEH* is spelled out in shiny gold thread.

She tucks a lacy handkerchief in my bag. "Now put on your gloves, and straighten up when you walk."

The lace gloves itch. It's hard to keep my balance in the new slippers. "Do I have to go? I don't know how to act at fancy doings."

"Oh, Primrose!" She pulls out a handkerchief and dabs at her eyes. "I've gone to all this trouble for you."

"But I didn't expect you to go to any trouble. I just wanted to spend some time with you." I'm not used to seeing grown folks cry. My stomach twists, and I swallow hard.

She sniffles and hunches her shoulders. "It-it's all right. Stay here if that's what you want. I'll go down *alone.*"

I push back a sigh. "I'll go if you want me to, but I won't know how to behave."

She whisks the handkerchief into her **reticule** and smiles. "Silly! Just do what I do."

We move down the steps to the big hall, which my mother calls the *lobby*. This time I'm the one who grips the banister. I hope we'll have a chance at supper to talk about the years we've been apart. Mama Lu holds that mealtimes give folks a good visiting space.

Dressed in a black suit and a shiny tie, Mr. Grayson waits at the dining room doors. "Good evening." He pulls the door open and sweeps his arm inside. "Right this way."

My mother nods and follows him. I stumble along behind on the red-and-gold carpet. The dining room is long and narrow. Three square tables line up on each side with walking room down the middle like the aisle at church. White cloths and candles in silver holders decorate the tables. A giant painting of a woman hangs on the far wall. I reckon it's supposed to be Virginia Dare, though folks believe she died when she was a little girl.

Four white-haired people sit around one table. A man who looks to be about Pa's age eats alone at another. He waves as we pass by. Mr. Grayson leads us to the last table on the right and pulls out a chair for my mother. I pull out my own. Our table is next to a big square of polished wood floor. A piano sits in one corner.

"For dancing later," my mother whispers. "We'll have such fun!"

Dancing? Before I can object, the boy named Titus comes to our table. He's dressed considerable better now, and his yellow hair's slicked back.

"Evening, ladies."

"Good evening, Titus." My mother smiles big at him. "I believe we'll have the special Virginia Dare birthday supper."

"Yes, ma'am."

As soon as he's out of hearing, I turn to my mother. "I don't know how to dance."

She giggles. "Silly! It's as easy as falling off a log."

I doubt she knows much about falling off logs.

While we wait for our food, she starts a conversation.

"Tell me all about yourself. Do you have a special beau?"

A beau? "I only just turned twelve today."

"It's never too soon to start thinking about settling down with someone special. Someone who will take care of you and give you fine things."

"I plan to take care of myself."

She gives out a high, silly laugh. "Oh, Primrose, you'll change your mind about that soon enough."

"Nope. I'm going to be a surfman like Pa."

Her laugh irritates me. "You know that can't happen! Girls aren't meant to do such hard work."

"It's hard," I agree, "but it's important."

"Of course it is, but so is living a beautiful, happy life."

"Pa and me and my brothers—we all have a happy life and—"

"Primrose, I know all about that life. I should think you'd want something better for yourself."

Before I can answer, Titus comes up carrying a tray

loaded with bread and two bowls of brown water. He puts a bowl in front of my mother. I get the other one.

"Oh, good. Bouillon! My favorite." She puts her napkin in her lap.

I do the same. I stare at the stuff. Too thin for gravy. Too hot to drink. I wait.

She picks up a big spoon and nods toward my plate.

That's when I notice that it's surrounded by enough eating tools for a whole family—spoons, forks, even two kinds of knives. Why on earth would a person need all that for one meal? Seems foolish, but I say nothing. This must be how fancy people do things.

She dips her spoon in the bowl and brings it to her mouth. I do the same. I can't taste much but salt and—

"Primrose! Don't slurp! Dip the spoon away from you! Sip!" she whispers at me from behind her napkin.

I scoot down in my chair. My cheeks burn. I stare at the salty brown water.

"Finished?" Titus points at my bowl.

I nod.

He replaces it with a little plate of lettuce and sliced tomatoes.

"Cut up the lettuce before you put it in your mouth," my mother warns me.

She gives orders all the way through the meal. When I pick up the piece of fried chicken, she gasps loud enough to turn every head in the room. "*What* are you doing? You *never, ever* eat with your fingers!"

I slouch so low that I'm about to slide onto the floor.

"Sit up straight. For heaven's sake, act like a lady. You're embarrassing me!"

I'm embarrassing *her*? I sit up and twist my napkin into a knot.

By the time dessert comes, I'm plumb worn out trying to do what she says. I've not eaten anything since breakfast, but every bite I take goes down in a lump. When I look at the slice of Virginia Dare's birthday cake covered by a mound of vanilla ice cream, I feel quamished.

I stumble out of my chair and run from the dining room.

TWENTY-SIX

whopperjawed—*out of place; crooked*

Without thinking, I race across the lobby and out the hotel's front door. There's no one on the porch, so I drop into a chair. Bending over, I take deep gulps of fresh air. Slowly, my stomach calms, and I let loose the sobs that have built up ever since I set foot in that dining room. Ever since I stepped off the mailboat.

"Are you sick?"

I've hoped that my mother would come to look after me. Instead, she's sent Titus. More embarrassment. I straighten up. Smooth my dress. Shake my head.

"Your mother thought you'd want to go to your room." He holds out the key.

"Thank you." I close my hand around it so tight that I can feel every ridge.

He shuffles his feet. "Uh, well, I'd best get back to my work."

"Go ahead." I prefer my own company to his—or my mother's. I kick off my slippers and sit a while longer in the cooling night. Roses climb a trellis at the end of the porch, and I walk over to enjoy their fragrance.

Soon I hear piano music. My mother is probably dancing now. Maybe with the man who waved as we passed by his table. I pound the porch railing as hard as I can. My mother should be on Whisper Island, dancing with my father! Living in our little cottage with me and my brothers. Not traveling around having a fine, fancy time wherever she goes.

Carrying my slippers, I walk back inside and cross the lobby. I look straight ahead and hurry up the stairs. At Room 213, I turn the key in the lock. We left the room in a mess. Everything is **whopperjawed**. My surprise pink dress has slipped off the chair onto the floor. Wads of crumpled wrapping paper are scattered across the bed covers.

I long to kick everything around and make a worse mess, but that would lead to more scolding. Mama Lu would caution me not to go to sleep in an unkempt room, so I set to work.

I clear the bed of wrapping paper scraps and hang the dress in the wardrobe. One hair clip sparkles on the windowsill. After a search, I find the other one under the bed, and I look for the leather box where my mother keeps her clips. It's on the reading table by the armchair. The ribbons and clips are in a right mess. When I go to straighten them, everything tumbles out in a tangle. A layer of papers rests on the bottom of the case. My name is written in thick, bold letters on the top sheet.

Why is it in her box? I pull it out so that I can see the whole note.

A gift for my granddaughter, Primrose Estella Hopkins.
From Theodore Whitney

My fingers tremble so hard that I nearly tear the paper. It awes me to think that I'm holding something from my grandfather. I unfold the paper and find a note inside.

August 1, 1913
Dear Rose Alene,
I have given you many chances to make things right with your daughter, but you have failed to do so.
Three months ago I told you that if you did not re-establish contact with Primrose, I would stop your allowance.

I tried to make up for your mother's death by giving you whatever you wanted, but I could not agree to your marriage. Sam Hopkins is an honorable, kind man, but I knew that life on Whisper Island would not be to your liking.

I cannot undo what has already happened, but you are thirty-one and old enough to assume some responsibility toward your own child.

I have enclosed this money for Primrose's twelfth birthday. See that she receives it. If you choose not to meet with her, send her the money by mailboat.

Your father,
Theodore A. Whitney

There's too much to take in. My grandfather knows how old I am. My own mother grew up without a mother. My grandfather thinks my father is an honorable man.

I peel off my stockings and lie back on the bed to read my grandfather's words again and again. I'm worn out from all that's happened. I reach over and turn off the bedside lamp. I'm too tired to bother taking off Mama Lu's dress and the rest of my new finery. Still clutching the letter, I fall asleep.

"Get up!" My mother shakes my shoulder.

I sit up and rub my eyes. "Wh-what time is it?"

The clock reads one o'clock. I can't remember ever being awake past midnight.

"What are you doing with my personal correspondence?" She snatches the letter from me.

"I was straightening up and putting things away. I saw my name on a note and so I read it." I wonder if she'll mention the money that should have been there.

She says nothing, but her face turns red, as if she's also thinking about that money. "That was *my* letter. You had no right to go poking in my things!" She puts the letter in her reticule and marches into the bathroom, slamming the door behind her.

Although the sound of her weeping fills me up with sadness, I know that I will leave in the morning. I've spent enough time with my mother.

TWENTY-SEVEN

whipstitch—*every now and then*

When my mother comes out of the bathroom, it's nearly two o'clock. She crosses the room in a silvery gray nightdress that's as fancy as her daytime clothes.

"I suppose you want to know where your money is."

"No, ma'am."

"Humph! Don't lie to me."

My fists tighten under the sheet. "I didn't come here for money."

She shrugs. "The money's gone. I spent it all on you."

I stare at her. "On fancy things I've no use for."

Her handkerchief comes out again. "I was only trying to do something nice for you." She slumps on her side of the bed and sobs.

Another memory comes:

Someone sits on a big bed with me. Her tears fall on my shoulders. "I can't live here. It's too hard!"

My mother walks into the bathroom again. The memory disappears. I pull up the covers and turn my back. Though I'm upset and hungry, I'm so tired that sleep comes quickly.

The next morning, I wake early and slip into the bathroom to wash up and brush my hair. I put on my Persian Pickle dress. A quick look in the mirror tells me I look fine. I'll go back across the Sound in style. Mama Lu's style. *My* style! After I lace up my black shoes, I stuff all my gifts into the carpetbag. Though I've no use for them, they're the only gifts I've ever received from my mother.

She sleeps soundly, one arm hanging off the edge of the bed, and snores softly—not loud and ragged like Pa or my brothers. I pick up my carpetbag and tiptoe across the room. When I bump my foot against the bedpost, she turns over and stretches. I stand as still as the naked lady statue downstairs, hoping she won't wake up. Finally, she turns onto her side and faces away from me.

I write a note on a scrap of the gold-and-silver wrapping paper and place it on the reading table.

> *Dear Mother,*
> *I am going back to Whisper Island. Thank you*
> *for the gifts, especially the beautiful retticyool.*
> *Your daughter,*
> *Primmy*

I reckon I should say something more flowery and sign it with "love," but I'm bent on honesty. I don't feel any true love for my mother. This fact makes me sad. And angry. I hoped we'd get acquainted. Promise to stay in touch and meet again. It's plain that Rose Alene can't live up to such a promise, even in a **whipstitch** way.

I tiptoe to the door. The hallway is dark, and I walk carefully down the stairs. No one stirs in the lobby. No sour-looking man. No Mr. Grayson or Titus. I open the front door and ease it shut behind me. The sun hasn't begun to heat up the day. On the porch I stop to breathe in the cool morning air. A soft wind makes it perfect for crossing the Sound.

I make my way past the houses and shops along the hotel's street. A horse-drawn wagon clip-clops toward me and goes on toward the Virginia Dare. As it passes, I see DAWSON'S MILK spelled out in big green letters. The driver waves. "G'morning, miss."

He and I are the only two people about.

At the end of the street, I turn and walk to the dock. A small barrel marked NAILS is just the right height for sitting. Several fishing boats dot the Sound. The mail-boat hasn't yet arrived from Whisper Island. It won't make its return trip until mid-afternoon. A long time to wait, but I have no other choice.

My stomach growls loudly to remind me that I've had little to eat since yesterday morning. I smile, thinking how the rumblings would embarrass my mother. I wish I had a bit of the money my grandfather sent. I'd buy myself a tasty meal, though I don't know where to find one. My empty belly will have to make do.

I pull down my hat brim and slump against a post.

"*Klöbchen!*" a familiar voice wakes me.

"Oh, Herr Bachmeier!" I clutch his arm. I'm so happy to see someone from home that my tears pour out.

Herr Bachmeier pats my back while I cry. We stay that way for a long while. When my tears slow, he bends down to wipe them away with his handkerchief.

"I want to go home. To Whisper Island."

He nods, but before he can say something, my stomach grumbles.

He laughs softly and pats his middle. "*Der Magen* speaks! We must find a place to eat." He gives me his hand. "Come. We will have a good meal, and you can tell me about your unhappiness—if you wish."

He leads me along the dockside street until we come to a corner sign: *Seaman's Café*. An arrow tells us to turn right.

"This will do." Herr Bachmeier holds the door open and motions me inside.

We sit at a table by the dingy front window, and Herr Bachmeier tells the cook what we want. Soon I look at hot cakes. Fried eggs. Sausage. Biscuits and gravy. And a big glass of milk. One fork, one spoon, and a knife wait for me to dig in.

I eat fast and noisily, just like Pansy. My mother would no doubt disapprove of my manners. I stop chewing to pour more sorghum over the buckwheat cakes.

Herr Bachmeier smiles at me across the table. "You are fine now? No more grumbling from *Der Magen*?"

"Thank you. *Danke*." I take another bite and lean back against my chair. "I feel better."

"And now we have a wait before we return to Whisper Island. The mailboat will dock soon, and we can board after Homer unloads. It will be more comfortable to wait on the boat."

"Good!" I want to leave Cranston as soon as I can.

Herr Bachmeier takes a bite of egg.

"Can I ask you something?" I spoon gravy on a biscuit.

"Of course, *Liebchen*."

I tell him about my grandfather's letter. "What is he like?"

TWENTY-EIGHT

slick cam—*very calm water*

Herr Bachmeier reaches across the table to pat my hand. "I have known Theodore Whitney a long time. A good man, but unhappy. Unhappy with your mother. Perhaps most of all unhappy with himself. He wishes he had done things in a different way after your grandmother died."

My grandmother.

"She passed away before she could even hold her baby girl. Your grandfather hired a nurse to raise his little daughter." Herr Bachmeier stares out at the street. "He had no family to help him."

I think about Mama Lu and how she helped Pa.

"I worked for your grandfather, running his clam factory on Whisper Island. Gerda and I were Rose Alene's godparents. We offered to care for her, but your grandfather wanted her to grow up in Boston."

I set my fork on the table. "If he didn't want her to come to Whisper Island, how did she meet Pa?"

"When your mother was eighteen, she decided to surprise her father for his birthday. She traveled to Whisper Island on a merchant ship. Theodore was surprised—and angry. But he agreed to let her stay for a time with Gerda and me. Then he left to start a new business in Charleston."

He takes another sip of coffee.

"Gerda took your mother to see the Life-Saving Station one day when your father was on duty." He smiles. "Your mother was beautiful. Your father invited her to a dance. It was—there is a saying—ah, yes! It was love at first sight."

I picture them at the dance and another memory comes:

She holds me and hums a tune. My father swoops us up, and we whirl around and around.

The cook interrupts the dancing memory. "Anything else?"

"More coffee, *bitte*." Herr Bachmeier goes on. "Your mother always got her way. But when she wanted to marry Sam Hopkins, her father said no." He stirs a spoonful of sugar into his coffee. "A few weeks later, your parents were married in our little church. She was a beautiful bride. She carried roses, and my Gerda made a photograph of her."

The picture in my Bible.

"If my grandfather knows where I am, why doesn't he write me?"

Herr Bachmeier finishes his coffee. "He is proud. More stubborn than your mother. He never admits to a mistake. It is easier for him to say that your mother is wrong."

I think about all this while I clean my plate.

After Herr Bachmeier pays for our breakfast, he picks up my carpetbag, and we walk back to the dock to watch for the mailboat.

While we wait, I tell him everything that's happened since I left Whisper Island. From Martha soiling my skirt to my mother's gifts and the Virginia Dare supper calamity. I end with my biggest complaint. "She laughed when I said I wanted to be a Life-Saver. Said I should learn to be a lady."

Herr Bachmeier pats my hand. "Ah, but you *are* a lady, Primmy. A kind, thoughtful young woman."

The sun's nearly overhead when the mailboat docks. This trip, Martin Forrest leads a milk cow down the ramp.

Several people follow, some carrying crates of vegetables and squawking hens. Miz Cullen waves to somebody on the dock and hurries off with her two little boys.

Homer Clackhunt walks toward us. "Cut your visit short, Primmy? Hope everything went all right." It's clear he wants to hear what happened. I say nothing.

He turns to Herr Bachmeier. "Take care of your business, Gus?"

Instead of answering, my friend picks up my carpetbag. "I think we will wait in the cabin, out of the sun."

Homer shrugs. "Suit yourself. It'll be near two hours afore I head back. The Sound is **slick cam** today. Should be a smooth trip over to the island."

I'm happy to hear that. My full belly is content, and I have no desire to upset it. Inside, I sit on the bench next to Herr Bachmeier and puzzle over the talk between the two men.

"Why did Homer ask about your business?"

"Ach! He wants to know everyone's news. I went to Cranston to settle an important matter. Can I trust you to keep a secret?"

"Oh, yes!"

"I'm the new Wreckmaster for Whisper Island. Your father asked me to do this when Uly Hacklin moved away last spring. You must not say anything yet."

I promise to keep the news to myself. A yawning

fit overcomes me, and I gladly accept Herr Bachmeier's offer to use his folded jacket as a pillow.

"Where is she?'

My mother's voice breaks into my sleep. I jump up and see that I'm alone. The sound comes from outside.

Herr Bachmeier answers. "She is asleep, Rose."

"Poppa Gus, I didn't mean to make her run away."

My heart pounds as I listen to her sobs.

"I know. You would not be unkind on purpose. Perhaps it is better to leave now. Plan to see her again next year."

"I'll write her."

"Yah. That is a good idea."

My mother's sobs slow. "Do you think she'll write back?"

"Primmy is a good girl who would like to know you. But you must take the first step."

"I'll try, Poppa Gus."

"Auf Wiedersehen, Rose."

I look out the little window above the bench and see my mother. My chest tightens, and I choke back tears. I long to run outside and tell her good-bye.

But she turns the corner and is gone.

TWENTY-NINE

newfangled—*brand new; original*

We get a late start because Homer waits for Mr. Poston, the traveling toothbrush salesman, to appear. I'm itching to get back home, and the delay irritates me no end.

We finally get underway—without Mr. Poston—and enjoy a smooth journey across the Sound. A light wind pushes us along in good time, and we dock at Whisper Island near suppertime.

I step onto the island and breathe in the crisp smell of the island pines. The ocean's salt air tickles my nose. Gulls and terns squawk at one another as they circle the dock, looking for food. I take off my shoes and enjoy the cool softness of the sandy path.

I'm home.

Herr Bachmeier walks with me as far as Mama Lu's. He hands over the carpetbag and tips his hat. *"Auf Wiedersehen*, Primmy."

"Thank you for everything. You are very kind. I'll see you for Thursday supper."

"Danke. Until then." He walks off down the path.

Mildred and Mortimer circle my legs as I step onto Mama Lu's porch. I bend to pet them and then knock on the door. "Yoo-hoo! I'm home."

She comes to the door, wiping her hands on a towel. "Land sakes, child. You're back a day early." She looks hard at me. "Come in and tell me all about it. Was there trouble?"

"Some." I step inside. After a long hug, I tell her the hard parts of my trip first. I end with Herr Bachmeier's kindness and my mother's last minute try at making peace.

Mama Lu shakes her head. "Shame it turned out so hard, Primmy. I feared it might."

I relax against her shoulder. "It's good to be back where folks eat normal and wear reasonable clothes." I tell her about the strange dress my mother wore when I first met her. "It bubbled out like a balloon and then came in tight below her knees. She could creep along no faster than an inchworm."

I demonstrate my mother's walk.

Mama Lu laughs. "Glory! That must have been a sight. Rose Alene always did favor any **newfangled** thing that came along."

We chat a while longer, and then I walk to our cottage. Edwin's out back feeding Pansy, and I sneak up on him. "Guess who?"

He jumps back from the fence, dropping a pan of scraps into the pen. "Primmy! What're you doin' home so soon?"

I tell him some of what went on. "Mostly I just missed everybody here—even Pansy."

Edwin smiles. "Likely Pansy missed you too. She gets lonely, you know, if no one's around. Come on in and eat with me. I fixed up a mess of greens and ham hocks. Mama Lu sent some cornbread."

"Sounds mighty fine. I missed plain cooking. Food's too fancy in Cranston." I tell him about the Virginia Dare supper.

He makes a face. "Doesn't seem like much of a meal to me."

After supper I want to go see Pa, but Edwin advises against it. "This time of night, he'll be busy writing the day's report. Wait 'til morning."

Probably just as well. I'm plumb worn out from my trip. Edwin offers to do the washing up and sends me off to bed.

I hang my two dresses on pegs and leave the rest of my belongings in the carpetbag. I put my mother's wedding photograph back in the Bible. "Good night, Mama." I go to sleep wondering if that's what I called her before she left me.

"Primmy! Primmy Hopkins!"

I'm still asleep when I hear two noisy boys at the door. They bang and whistle.

"All right. I'm coming." I pull on my trousers and shirt.

The two of them stand on the porch with their noses about to poke a hole clear through the screen.

"Edwin told us you were home. We thought you wasn't coming back until today," Emory says.

"Well, here I am, no matter what you thought."

"Why're you back so early?" Will asks.

Instead of answering, I tell them the parts of my trip I know they'll marvel at.

They especially like the bit about Martha spraying her breakfast all over my skirt.

"Didn't that make you sick too?" Emory asks. "I always want to join in when folks air their paunch." He grins. "That's what cowboys say when someone throws up."

"A right good way to put it," Will says.

I frown. "Mayhap. Whatever you call it, it's not pleasant."

When I tell them about all the forks and spoons and whatnot, they shake their heads.

"Naw," Will says. "That can't be right. Who needs all that to eat a meal?"

I explain as best I can. "There's one fork for this and one for that, a big spoon for soup and another to stir sugar into coffee. My mother ate her salad with a little fork and—"

"Does your ma let you have coffee too?" Emory sure is fixed on the idea of having himself some coffee.

"I left before they served it," I admit.

"Left?" Will says.

When I explain, he turns serious. He pats my arm. "I'm sorry, Primmy. You must feel bad at how everything went. I'm real sorry."

Emory starts in wriggling—a sure sign that things are too quiet and lacking in excitement. "Come on, let's go over to the beach and look for treasure."

I shake my head. "I haven't seen Pa yet. After I eat breakfast, I'm going to the station."

"We'll go with you," Emory says.

Will pulls his friend toward the door. "We'd best be

going. Primmy wants to see her pa alone. We'll catch up
with her later."

"But—"

Emory doesn't get to finish before Will's got him
outside and down the path.

I stand at the door and stare after them. Will's turned
real thoughtful. What's come over him?

I pour myself some milk and finish last night's
cornbread.

Then I set out to see Pa.

THIRTY

slumgullion—*watery meat stew*

Deep gray thunderheads march in from the southeast toward Whisper Island. My walk to the station is hard, slow work. The air smells like rain.

Herr Bachmeier is standing outside the cookhouse with Pa. My father looks right handsome in his dark blue uniform. Its brass buttons gleam, even in the dim sunlight.

"I would like to begin at once, Sam."

"The sooner the better, Gus," Pa says.

"'Morning." I smile at the two men.

"Primmy!" Pa looks me over. "Gus told me you came over with him last night." He shakes hands with Herr Bachmeier. "You'll make a fine Wreckmaster, my friend."

"*Danke.*" Herr Bachmeier bows. "I must go now. *Auf Wiedersehen.*"

I follow Pa to the cookhouse and sit at the table.

Pa pours us some coffee. "Sorry things went hard for you over there." He nods toward the Sound. "Gus told me about your fancy new clothes and the highfalutin dinner."

I'm glad Herr Bachmeier saved me having to tell Pa about my trip. "That dinner was right troublesome. Fancy food. None of it tasted like much, in my opinion. I coulda stayed in my room and chewed on brown paper!"

Pa laughs and hugs me close. "I missed you, Primmy. Thought about you the whole time. Wondered how things were going between you and your ma. Glad you decided to come back home to us."

I stare at him. How could he think I'd leave him and go off with my mother? "She told Herr Bachmeier that maybe we could meet up again next summer."

Pa mumbles something, but I can't make it out. He looks out at the ocean for a long while and then clears his throat. "How's your ma getting along, Primmy?"

"She's fine, Pa. She gave me a real fancy purse for my birthday. To go with my new dresses."

"She always had an eye for pretty things." His voice cracks like something's stuck down deep, and he looks back out the window. "It's time for signal flag practice. You'd best get along. We'll talk more later."

I hug him hard and long. "It's good to be home!"

His hand shakes when he holds the screen door open for me. "It's fine to have you back. Come by after church Sunday and we'll have us a long chinwag. Jacob should be around too, before he starts beach patrol."

I'm just past Mama Lu's when she calls me from her porch.

"Lou Connor came by, askin' if you want some windfall peaches," she says. "You can keep whatever you pick up. Monday's blow loosened 'em off their stems."

I've just slung a sack over my shoulder when Will and Emory appear.

"Where ya going?" Emory asks.

When I tell him, he grins big. "Peaches! I sure do like peaches."

Will snorts. "They're probably all moldy by now. Pansy's the only critter I know who'll eat rotten food."

Boys have no idea about much of anything. "Not rotten. Just on the ground for a day. I can make all manner of things with windfall fruit."

The boys take a sack and follow me down the lane to the Connor place. Peaches cover the ground. Bees swarm around the smashed fruit, and I wave them away.

Will appears to have forgotten what he said about Pansy. He and Emory eat more than they stow in their sack. When they're not stuffing themselves, they look for squashed fruit to slide around on. By the time I've half-filled my sack, they're covered with peach mess.

"Emory, your aunt's gonna skin you when she sees those peach stains," I say.

"Naw, they'll wash right out," he insists.

I'm about to caution Will when Emory gives a mighty scream.

"Yeow! I been stung!"

His lip swells up, and it's clear he must have tried to take the same bite a bee was after.

He's hopping all over so much he's riling up any other bees that might be buzzing around. Before I can grab him, he takes off for home. Bees follow.

Will goes after him. "I'd best see if he's all right."

I stay put and fill my sack.

Mama Lu and I spend Thursday morning making peach butter. I save the best chunks to make a cobbler for Herr Bachmeier's supper.

He arrives right on time. As we eat, it comes to me that he and I are friends. I used to think he was just a funny old man who pushed his moustache back when he ate. Now I know him to be kind and wise.

"Fine meal," Edwin says. "Herr Bachmeier, you're lucky that Primmy came back in time to fix our supper.

If I'd been the cook, you'd be stuck with a sad plate of **slumgullion**."

"Primmy is a talented young woman."

My cheeks burn. I fumble with my hair. Gulp down some milk.

Edwin passes the sweet potatoes to our guest. "Pa's real happy that you're going to be working with him."

"Yah. I am eager to start."

"Wreckmaster's a good job for you. You'll take right good care of the property left from a wreck."

Herr Bachmeier beams. "*Danke*, Edwin. I also want to help the survivors."

A happy idea comes to me. No rule says females can't work with a Wreckmaster!

"I'd like to help you." My stomach flutters at the prospect.

Edwin groans. "Wreckmaster work isn't fitting for a girl, no more'n life-saving."

"There must be something I can do." I cross my arms and narrow my eyes at my brother.

Herr Bachmeier smiles at me. "I think you will discover what that is, Primmy."

I know I will!

THIRTY-ONE

whit—*a bit of time*

Friday morning, I help Mama Lu make cactus jelly. Even though we start early, it's so hot that we barely notice the heat rising from the canning pots. Afterward we move to the porch to enjoy a cool drink and catch any breeze that might come our way. Mildred and Mortimer creep out from under the porch to join us.

"I'm sure pleased about Gustave being our new Wreckmaster." Mama Lu sips/ her lemonade. "He'll likely use the old clam factory for storage and then hold vendues there to sell off the salvage."

"I'm going to help him." I tug Mildred onto my lap. She's heavier than ever. Another litter must be about ready.

Mama Lu raises her eyebrows and peers at me

over her glasses. "What kind of help might you be offering?"

"Not sure yet, but just give me a **whit.** I'm working on a plan."

Mama Lu sighs. "Primmy, your plans lead to problems more often than not. Be sure of what you're doing."

"Yes, ma'am." Nobody thinks I can do a blessed thing without causing trouble!

Next day, the boys and I scout the beach for treasure. Will and I try to stay upwind of Emory. His aunt covered his bee stings with onion slices, and he still smells of the treatment. He chatters away about watching the Thursday life-saving drills. "Pap and Jacob worked with the life car. I sure would hate to get shut up in one of them contraptions!"

I shudder. I suppose folks on a sinking ship might be so scared that they wouldn't mind being locked up in a life car and hauled to shore. Lying flat in a closed metal container seems too much like being in a coffin. "The breeches buoy looks more comfortable. Folks can step in like it's a pair of pants and hold on to the life ring while they swing to shore."

Emory agrees and then shifts his talk. "Today's prob'ly the last time we can look for treasure. Herr Bachmeier's gonna scoop up everything soon as there's a shipwreck."

"Naw," Will says. "There'll always be bits of this 'n that to find."

"Will's right." I pick up a piece of polished green glass and stuff it in my overall pocket. "His job is to save valuables and lumber from wrecked ships."

Emory shrugs and runs off in his harum-scarum manner, legs and arms flying every which way. Gulls fly away with angry squawks. Then he stops so sudden that sand sprays out from the sides of his feet. "Found me another one!" He holds up a horseshoe crab shell, the second one he's found this summer.

That boy sure has a treasure-finding talent.

"Gotta show Aunt Marcelle!" He gallops away.

Emory's out of sight by the time Will and I reach the path. We slow our pace.

Will stops to face me. Clears his throat. "What's your ma like?" he asks out of the clear blue. "Been wondering how you two got on. You've not said one word about it."

"Nothing to tell." I move faster.

Will comes right after me. "Musta been hard to see your ma after so long. Is that why you came back early?"

"I don't care to talk about it. My ma's right pretty. No need for you to know anything else." I hear the rudeness in my voice and set my mouth firm against saying more.

Will's face turns so red that his freckles disappear.

"Seems like you learned some bad manners from your ma." He stomps off into the woods.

I watch him disappear and wonder when I'll see him again. I regret acting so ugly, but I'm not used to such private questions. I'm surely not comfortable trying to answer them.

I take the cemetery path and spend close to an hour attacking weeds. I take extra care around Gerda Bachmeier's grave. As I work, I try to sort out why Will's attentions get me so riled, but no answer comes.

After supper, Edwin leaves to call on Katrina. My new hat's squashed from all its travels, so I take it, along with clean drawers and vest, to Mama Lu's for my Saturday bath. We haul the metal tub into the kitchen. While the water heats, I show her my poor hat.

"I've tried to make it round again, but it just folds back on itself."

"I know a trick that just might work." Mama Lu soaks a rag in water and pats it all around my hat. It droops worse than ever.

I can't picture it ever resembling a hat again.

"Stop frowning so." She sets a smallish mixing bowl on the table. "This should be 'bout right." She turns the bowl upside down and presses my hat onto it. "It'll be fine for church-going."

Next morning, I put on the blue dress, snatch up my

reticule, and run to Mama Lu's. My hat sits on her table, round and crisp as if it had just come from a fancy store. Its blue ribbons are smooth.

"Elspeth Thornton will be jealous!" I swing the reticule from side to side.

Mama Lu frowns. "Primmy, you have a tendency to think just one way about people. Elspeth lives in a big house and had a fancy do for her birthday, but that doesn't mean she's not worth knowing. Elspeth might be happy that you have such a fine hat."

I snort at this notion. "She even thinks she's too good to go to school with the rest of us."

"Do you think Elspeth just decided to stay home and make her ma teach her?"

"No, ma'am," I mutter.

"You'd best voice kinder thoughts about others whilst you sashay your way to church."

When Reverend Sewell starts to preaching, I'm sure Mama Lu's sent word that I need to hear his words about Mark 11:25–26. The reverend goes on and on about how I should forgive folks. That if I can't overlook the failings of others, I have no business expecting God to wink at my faults.

I am not happy with this news. It surely means that I'm obliged to overlook my mother's frippery. Elspeth's uppitiness. Will's peculiar behavior of late. Even the

Lavender sisters' holier-than-thou snootiness. Seems like way too much forgiving for one person. More than I have in me.

When we file out into the August heat, Mama Lu stops to thank Reverend Sewell. "Fine words. Inspiring." She nudges me forward.

I stand right in front of the reverend, eye-to-eye with the middle button of his preacher's coat. I know Mama Lu expects me to add to her praise.

"It was right nice," I mumble.

"Thank you, Primmy. You're doing a good job with the cemetery weeds. I believe I owe you six cents." He reaches in his pocket and hands over six pennies.

Elspeth and her ma step up as I'm putting the coins in my reticule.

"Oh, Primmy, what a beautiful purse!" Elspeth gushes.

"It's a reticule."

Another nudge from Mama Lu. Harder this time.

I work up a smile. "Thank you. It was a birthday present."

When Reverend Sewell asks Mama Lu and Miz Thornton about the Ladies Guild potluck supper, Elspeth pulls me aside.

"You're so lucky."

I stare at her.

"Getting to cross the Sound, all by yourself. Pa would *never* let me do that. He hardly lets me leave the house, 'cept for church."

"Come, Elspeth. It's time we get home." Her mother keeps us from further conversation.

"Looked like you and Elspeth had a good visit," Mama Lu says.

"I s'pose."

Could she be right about Elspeth having a nicer side?

THIRTY-TWO

bamboozle—*to trick or deceive*

From church, I head for the station. Sea oats bend in the wind as I walk along the path. I'm eager to tell Pa how I want to help Herr Bachmeier.

Pa's waiting for me at the station door. He eyes my reticule. "Mighty fancy bag you've got there, Primmy. Must be from your ma."

I don't point out its proper name. Correcting Elspeth is one thing. Pointing out my father's mistake is a different matter.

A gust of wind bangs the shutters as I step inside. "Seems like bad weather's blowing up."

"It'll likely be coming and going all day," Pa says. "We'll be busy."

I look around. "Where is everyone?"

"Jacob's in the lookout tower, and the rest are on their way to the station."

Usually the men spend Sunday with their families, but today the weather's calling them to work early.

"Mayhap I'd best go."

"Stay long enough to have some coffee."

I sit down and tell him my plan. "Herr Bachmeier wants to help out the folks who come off a wrecked ship. So, after we clean up the factory, we'll collect clothes and such from the village."

Pa frowns. "You've thought up a load of work for yourself, Primmy. You're right capable, but that's a lot to take on."

"The boys will help." I haven't asked them, but I hope that's true.

Pa sighs. "Have you talked to Gus about it?"

"Not yet, but I know he'll like my plan."

"It's a mighty nice idea, Primmy, but it's too much for a girl."

I glare at my father. "I'm an islander, Pa! I'm up to it. Do you want me to grow up to be a fancy lady like my mother?"

He slams his mug on the table. "Watch your sass, Primrose!"

I push back tears. "Sorry, Pa. I didn't mean to—"

Before I can finish, Justice Sperry and the Stiles

brothers come in. Pa starts going over their duties, and I slip away, unhappy with how I've left things. Yesterday I offended Will. Today my own father.

I run home to make a pros and cons list for my plan:

> *Pro—I can help when there's a shipwreck.*
> *Con—I'd be in for a lot of hard work.*
> *Pro—I could repay Herr Bachmeier for his kindness to me.*
> *Con—I can't quit when it gets hard.*
> *Con—Pa doesn't think it's a good idea.*
> *Con—Mama Lu agrees with Pa.*

I look over the list and sigh. Pros and cons rules say you should follow whichever side has the longest list. Mine has more cons than pros, but rules can be broken if there's a good reason. I have a good reason: I want to do this.

I rush through Monday wash chores and hurry to Emory's cottage. Miz Hoover's hanging out her sheets in the side yard. She waves.

"Emory's over to Will's place. You can catch up with 'em before they get up to much mischief."

I cut through the woods to the Cooper house. I

hope that Will's willing to forgive the mean words that slipped out of me a couple of days ago.

The boys are shooting marbles in the dirt.

"Hey!" I jump out of the woods the way Emory is fond of doing.

"Hey," Will mumbles. He's just knuckled down to take aim. Emory sits back on his heels and waits for the shot.

I sigh. Talking to the back of someone's head is no good. I step closer. My bare toe hits the line that marks their playing circle.

"Drat!" Will explodes. "Whaddya do that for?"

"I want to talk to the two of you."

Will pokes his finger into the dirt and redraws the line. "We're busy."

"This is important. Please!"

He still won't look at me. "Wait till we're done."

I sigh. A marble game can take all afternoon. "No! This is exciting. Dangerous!"

This gets Emory's attention. "What is it? Huh?" He jumps up and disturbs the marbles still in the circle.

"Oh, double drat!" Will scoops up his winnings. "Game's over—thanks to you!"

"Tell us." Emory pockets his marbles and pulls on my shirt sleeve.

"It's a plan to help Herr Bachmeier with his new job."

Will groans. "Why are you so bent on doing man's work?"

"Just listen. He wants to use the old clam factory, and we can help him clean it up."

"Cleaning?" Emory squeals. "I ain't much for scrubbing."

"It's a lot more than scrubbing. There's broken glass to clear up. Doors to be repaired. Walls to scrape and paint." I hope this list will seem more *manly* and will **bamboozle** my two friends into helping.

Emory grins. "When do we start?"

Will doesn't say anything.

"Let's go talk to Herr Bachmeier," I say.

Emory and I head for the harbor. Will follows. I can barely hear his mumble.

"If I help, it'll be for Herr Bachmeier. Not for you."

THIRTY-THREE

a lick and a promise—*haphazard; careless*

Our new Wreckmaster stands in the factory office, a square room in a front corner of the building. He smiles when he sees us.

"*Guten Morgen!*"

We each answer in German as best we can. Emory and I step right in, but Will hangs back on the doorstep.

I explain why we've come. Herr Bachmeier smiles and now and then lifts his eyebrows. I'm getting to the part about collecting clothes from the villagers when he holds up his hand.

"You are very kind, but this will be difficult. I think perhaps you must be sure of your parents' permission."

On the way home, I ask Will if he's going to help.

"I don't know." He rushes on ahead and disappears.

Turns out that Will's ma and Emory's aunt say yes. Afraid Pa might say no, I ask Edwin at supper. "Fine idea," he says.

We report for duty next morning and start on the office area. By noon, we're dirty and tired. Sweat runs down my back. My arms ache from reaching high to scour the storage shelves. We finish the office room, except for scrubbing the floor.

"You have done good work, my friends," Herr Bachmeier says. "Now I think you must go home and rest."

I'm happy to agree.

Will turns up late the next day with a complaint. "I thought we were going to scrape and paint."

I'm about to answer when Elspeth Thornton pokes her curly head in the doorway.

"Yoo-hoo!"

I sigh. What does *she* want?

"I heard you were working for Herr Bachmeier. Can I help?"

My mouth drops open at her offer. I try to picture Elspeth giving the place a good scrubbing. She seems more like **a-lick-and-a-promise** worker, but she appears serious about her offer.

I'm about to answer, when Herr Bachmeier comes in. He pats Elspeth's shoulder.

"Guten Morgen, Klöbchen."

What? That's Herr Bachmeier's special word for *me*. Elspeth's too skinny to be a dumpling!

Another surprise: Elspeth agrees to scrub the floor. Doesn't she see the bird mess? The dark oily stains? Does she know she'll have to get down on her knees to get at all that ground-in dirt?

Will and Emory go outside to pick up broken glass, leaving me and Elspeth to work on the floor. Herr Bachmeier hands us each a brush, a cake of lye soap, and a bucket of water.

"Let's get started." Elspeth sounds cheery, like we're going to a party.

Instead of answering, I take my supplies to the doorway and scrub my way toward the farthest corner.

Some minutes later I find myself facing the wall, clean floor behind me and no place to go.

Elspeth giggles. "Silly. You've trapped yourself!"

When she says "silly," I hear my mother laughing at me. I was *silly* then because I didn't know what a reticule was. Now I'm *silly* because of the way I scrub floors.

Seems I can't do anything to suit other folks.

I can't be a proper lady like my mother wants. I

won't become Mrs. Something-or-Other just to please my menfolk. I'll never live up to Reverend Sewell's sermons or Mama Lu's advice. And no matter what I do, the Lavender sisters would still like me to disappear.

I stand up and stomp toward the door. And slip on the wet wood and sprawl onto my rump. Hard. I grit my teeth and wait for more laughter.

Instead, Elspeth rushes to my aid. I'm startled by her kindness.

"Are you all right?" She struggles to help me up, but I'm too much dumpling for her skinny little person, and she lands on the floor next to me. I expect screeches of dismay about her ruined clothes.

Elspeth gives me another surprise. She hugs me and falls back on the floor, pulling me with her. The two of us lie side by side, gawking at the cobwebby ceiling. No one thought to dust that high.

Giggling, Elspeth pulls on my arm. "Let's make snow angels," she says.

I turn to stare at her. "Snow *what?*"

"My cousins from Maine showed me how. You lie on the snow and move your arms and legs like this." She demonstrates. "It makes an angel shape in the snow." She giggles again. "We can be floor angels!"

A good way to get splinters on our backsides.

Before I can argue, she moves my arm up and down

along the floor. I fall into rhythm with her and soon I'm giggling too. This morning is filled with surprises.

Will and Emory come to the doorway.

Emory points his finger. "What're you two doing in here?"

"Making snow—" Elspeth can't get the words out between giggles.

"—angels!" I finish for her.

Emory plops himself down next to me. "Woo! This is fun. C'mon, Will, make a snow angel."

Will snorts. "Doesn't look to me like it has much to do with angels."

I watch him leave and wonder if I will ever feel like his friend again.

THIRTY-FOUR

betwixt and between—*in the middle; not entirely one thing or another*

We spend the next few mornings working on the factory building.

Will ignores me as much as possible and barely speaks. Elspeth shows up every morning and cleans alongside me while the boys work outdoors. On Thursday we finish the big room next to the office. It's big enough that shipwrecked folks can stay a day or two if need be.

At supper Thursday night, Herr Bachmeier cuts into the gooseberry pie Mama Lu sent for dessert. "You should be very proud of your sister," he tells Edwin. "She and her friends have done some very *diffizil* work this week. Your father is most pleased."

I gulp. "Pa knows?"

Edwin laughs. "There's not much on this island he *doesn't* know!"

My face burns.

Edwin goes on. "Pa knows more'n anybody about your stubborn streak. He wasn't surprised you went ahead. 'Course, he woulda preferred you got his approval."

Herr Bachmeier waves his hand over his plate. "No matter. He's proud of you—with good reason."

The next day, Herr Bachmeier greets us in front of the factory. "Reverend Sewell has found three men to help with the heavy work today." He looks at me. "Do you want to start the next part of your plan?"

"Yes!" I look at my friends.

Will frowns.

Elspeth smiles.

Emory's eyes light up. "What're we gonna do?"

I lay out the plan. "Talk to everyone in the village. Ask them for clothes. Shoes. Maybe towels and sheets. Whatever they can spare for folks who come through a bad wreck."

We decide to pair up and start with the houses near the harbor. Elspeth and I start out the door.

"I'll go with Elspeth," Will says. "Emory, you go with Primmy."

How long is Will going to stay mad at me?

"I'd rather go with Primmy," Elspeth says.

"Naw," Will says. "Better to have one boy and one girl team up."

There I stand, **betwixt and between** feelings. Angry at Will. Eager to get started.

"Let's go, Primmy!" Emory's out the door and half-way to Pepperdine's store.

I run to catch up. "Slow down. Let's think about what we're going to say."

"Think?" Emory says, like it's the strangest word he's ever heard. "We just go up and ask if they've got anything to help."

He's right. Most everyone already knows what we're doing and offers to bring something to the factory. Except for Mr. Pepperdine.

"I'm gonna put out a jar for money and some boxes for the things folks want to give," he says.

It doesn't take us long to finish, and we meet up with Will and Elspeth at the clam factory.

"What's next?" Elspeth asks.

"There's still a few houses on the ocean side," I say.

"We'll head north toward Hook Cove." Will starts off. "C'mon, Elspeth."

He's well on his way before I realize he's left Emory and me with Reverend Sewell. And the Lavender sisters.

"Do we hafta go there?" Emory whines. "Those two ladies don't like me one bit."

"They don't care for me, either, but we told Herr Bachmeier we'd see everyone on the island."

We visit the sisters first.

"Like eatin' your vegetables so you kin have dessert," Emory says. "Those two are surely not dessert."

I knock on the Lavender door. Emory crouches behind me.

Miz Hortense pulls it open and glares at me. "What do *you* want? Did you bring my parsnip money?"

"No'm. We're collecting goods for shipwreck victims."

"What's that got to do with me or my sister?'

"Folks might need clothes or shoes."

"Or books." Emory squeaks. "A good story can take your mind off your troubles."

Miz Hortense peers around me. "What are *you* doing here? Get off my porch!"

We both back down the steps. "If you think of anything you can spare, please leave it at Mr. Pepperdine's store!" I yell over my shoulder.

"Told-you-she-didn't-like-me," Emory pants as we run to Reverend Sewell's house.

Mrs. Sewell promises to leave supplies at the store. "And I'll make sure the Ladies Guild helps," she says.

Emory and I head back to the clam factory to report

on our work. We're just leaving Herr Bachmeier's office when Miz Pratt shows up with a bundle.

"Primmy! Wait up. I've gathered some things for you. Ginny would want you to have these for shipwrecked children." When she unfolds the bundle, little dresses and shoes tumble out, along with two dolls and a stuffed dog. "Can you use these?"

"Oh, yes! Thank you, Miz Pratt."

Later, as I walk toward home, I wonder what's become of Will and Elspeth.

THIRTY-FIVE

hobble skirt—*a skirt cinched so tight below
the knees that it makes walking difficult*

Edwin and Nate are in Cranston overnight looking for a new fishing boat, so I eat supper with
Mama Lu. Before I go to bed, I decide to donate my
birthday finery to the shelter. I'll keep my reticule.
Elspeth's admiration has helped me see it in a new
light.

Strong winds howl most of the night. By morning
they're some calmer. Even though gray clouds darken
the sky, I decide there's no need to close the shutters. I
hurry to the shelter early in hopes of having a word with
Will before we start work.

When I open the office door, I smile. A generous
villager has already been here. Two cots, a box of bed

linens, and a child's pull-toy are stacked against the far wall.

I'm folding sheets when Elspeth arrives. She drops a bag inside the door and holds out a basket of cookies. The sweet, sharp smell of ginger fills the air.

"Ma baked them this morning. They're real good." Elspeth bites into one. "She only makes them when Pa's away. He won't allow sweets in our house. Says they're bad for your health. Pa has rules for everything."

Living in a home with so many laws must wear on a person, always having to be good. Small wonder Elspeth seems snooty at times.

I sample a cookie. "How did you and Will get on yesterday?"

"Just fine."

"Emory and I waited for you two to come back."

Instead of answering, Elspeth reaches for a second cookie.

Polite talk is getting me nowhere, so I blurt out what I want to know. "How come you and Will didn't come back here when you finished?"

"It was time for my piano practice. Pa gets upset if I fall behind." She stops for a cookie bite. "Will went home to look after Rowena while his mother put up tomatoes."

I'm surprised at how this news pleases me. While I put my finery on a shelf, I tell Elspeth about the strange dress my mother wore. "She had to walk like this." I demonstrate.

Elspeth claps her hands. "Oh, I saw one on a funny postcard my uncle sent Pa. It's called a **hobble skirt**, but the card said it was a 'speed limit' skirt."

We laugh together, and I realize I don't mind a bit that Elspeth knows something I don't. A week ago I would've thought she was showing off.

She opens her bag and pulls out a stuffed bear, a set of blocks, and something I've never seen before.

"What's that?" I point to two wooden hoops, wrapped round and round with colored ribbons.

"A game of Graces. These go with it." She holds up four wooden sticks. "My cousins sent it for my birthday, but I've never had anyone to play it with."

For some reason, this makes me sad. Would she have invited me to play Graces if I'd been nicer? I'm about to ask about the game when Emory appears with a stack of books. He kicks the door shut behind him.

"It's getting dark out there. Say, what smells so good?' He makes a beeline for Elspeth's basket.

As Emory munches away, I look out the window. Will's coming up the path, pulling a wagon piled with goods.

I step outside into a gust of wind. "Hey."

Will nods.

I swallow hard. "Um—sorry I spoke mean the other day."

He shrugs. "Doesn't matter."

"But it *does* matter. We've been friends ever since I can remember."

"Maybe that's changed."

My face burns from his hurtful words, and I turn away.

"Hold up." Will touches my arm.

"Yes?" I hope he'll say we're still friends.

"Help me carry these inside."

I take the bundle of clothes. "These look like yours. How can you spare them?"

Another shrug. "Ma let my overalls down as far as they'll go." He grins—the first smile I've seen for a time. "She says I should stop growing for a year or two."

Will *has* grown. I have to lift my head to look him in the eye. Why haven't I noticed before?

I clear my throat. "Mighty nice of you to pass them on to the shelter."

He unloads a bag of marbles, a set of jackstraw pickup sticks, some of Rowena's baby clothes, and three jars of peach preserves. "Ma's got some put-up tomatoes and beans too. I'll bring 'em tomorrow."

"*Guten Morgen!*" Herr Bachmeier shows up with his

three helpers. All four men carry goods the villagers have left at Mr. Pepperdine's store.

Herr Bachmeier sets down his load. "I go now to the station to see about the weather. The sky does not look kind, and the fishing boats have come in." He rushes off, leaving his helpers to close the shutters against the wind. We hear their banging as we work.

Elspeth and I are stacking blankets into a trunk when Mrs. Thornton appears suddenly, as if the wind had blown her in.

"Elspeth! Come, we must get home before the storm hits." She grabs her daughter's arm. "Your father would never forgive me if something happened to you."

"But, Ma—" Elspeth is gone before she can finish her thought.

The wind and dark clouds can be sure storm signs, but Elspeth's ma could've waited a bit. At least 'til we finished with the blankets. I push hard to shut the door after them.

Herr Bachmeier hurries in before I can start back to work. "It is time for *der Kinder* to go home." He turns to me. "Your papa says a bad storm comes. The crew prepares for trouble."

"But we're not done," I protest. "A few more minutes won't matter."

"*Nein.* You must go." He holds the door open. "Now."

Emory steps outside. "Woo! That wind's picked up big. I gotta get home to put Furbit inside." He gallops off.

Herr Bachmeier frowns at Will and me. "You must go home."

Outside, black clouds roll in from the ocean. Wind gusts push the trees near to the ground, and blowing sand turns the air a hazy brown.

Will and I start down the path, bending into the wind. The sound of shutters being nailed into place grows fainter.

I turn to face Will. "You'd best get home to help your ma."

"I s'pose." Will takes the path to his house. "Take care, Primmy."

"You too, Will."

I continue on my way home. Sand cuts into my face like needles, and I cover my forehead to protect my eyes. I stop under an oak tree to get my bearings. About to move on, I hear men's shouts and horse hooves pounding on the surf—the sounds of Life-Savers on their way to a ship.

Now I can finally be of some use! I turn back toward the shelter.

THIRTY-SIX

flummoxed—*dazed; confused*

Before I go much farther, the storm calls up a hard rain to make things worse. Martha Crocker still has my oilskin, so my shirt and overalls are quickly soaked. I stumble along in the rising wind. When I stop to peer at the storm blowing in from the ocean, I see the sharp outline of a three-masted ship. Red flares light up the dark sky, signaling trouble. Probably run aground on a sandbar. Then battered by giant storm waves.

I turn away from the ocean and head back toward the shelter. Trying hard to keep my balance, I almost trip over something lying across the path. Most likely a fallen tree limb.

I'm about to step over but pull back in shock when I

see that it's Mr. Poston. "Mercy!" I lean over. The tooth-brush salesman lies on his side, moaning.

"Mr. Poston? Are you all right?"

He rolls onto his back and squints up at me. "No," he moans. "I tripped and hurt my foot."

"Is it broken?"

"I don't know," he wails. "I've lost my sample case."

I'm stuck for words when he voices more complaints. "My hat blew away. My shoes are full of sand."

"I'll get someone to help you. Just lie still." The near-est cottage belongs to the Lavenders. Drat! They'll never lend me a hand.

"No!" The little man's scream chills me. He clutches my shirt. "Don't leave me." For someone so **flummoxed**, he has a mighty grip. It's clear that he won't let me go until I agree to take him with me. There's no help for it. I'll have to knock on the Lavenders' door. While I work myself up to that fearsome task, I hear shouts from the beach.

I know that Pa's crew is pulling the beach cart into place on the sand. It's heavy with all the rescue equip-ment. Soon they'll shoot out a line from the Lyle gun and rig up the breeches buoy.

"You've got to help me," Mr. Poston whines.

This makes me somewhat prickly. I'm on my way to aid folks from the shipwreck. Stopping to help

Mr. Poston will keep me from real service to the Life-Savers.

I grit my teeth. "Can you stand up?"

More wails. "No!"

I struggle to roll him onto his hands and knees. "Lean on me and push yourself up."

He grunts and groans. Sags against me, pulling me down. Doesn't put one bit of effort into his own rescue.

I wish we were close to Mama Lu's cottage. She'd know what to do. But this is up to me—and the Lavenders.

I struggle on, pushing, prodding, and finally getting Mr. Poston on his feet. He hangs his full weight on my shoulders. My knees buckle and threaten to give way. "Listen here, Mr. Poston. If you want my help, you've got to do some of the work yourself. Straighten up as best you can and walk with me."

He uncurves himself a bit. "All right. I'll try."

Surfmen shout in the distance as Mr. Poston and I drag ourselves along. Wind and rain and Mr. Poston's limp posture slow us down, but we finally reach the Lavender place. The ocean's wind pushes at our backs as I struggle to the door and bang loud and long. The storm's roar muffles my knocking, but finally Miz Hortense pulls the door and holds it open just enough to see us.

"Oh. It's *you* making all that ruckus."

"Yes, ma'am. Please help us. Mr. Poston is hurt and needs to get in out of the storm."

"What's that to me?"

How can one woman be so uncaring? "Don't mean to be sassy, Miz Lavender," I growl, "but you know not one other person on this island would turn away someone in a storm, 'specially someone hurt bad."

"Humph!" Miz Hortense glares at me but opens the door. She disappears into the other room without a word. Chilled and wet, we step inside. A hearty fire crackles at us.

Mr. Poston collapses into a rocker by the fireplace. I stand beside him, wondering what to do next. My clothes drip onto the wooden floor. I shiver so hard that my teeth bang against each other.

For the first time, I have a clear view of Mr. Poston's foot. It's swollen up bad.

Some of Pa's first-aid lessons come back to me. Mr. Poston groans as I slip off his shoe and lift his foot onto a stool. "Keep it high," I order, "to help with the swelling."

The door swings open, and storm wind pushes Miz Aurelia inside. She takes off her slicker and hat and sits on a bench to pull off her waders. "My, that storm is fierce. Pity the surfmen have to be out in it."

A loud explosion rattles through the air. Pa has fired off the Lyle gun. The shot line is speeding to the ship. The life-saving work is underway. I long to help with the rescue. I've watched drills often enough that I could do anyone's job. Get the beach cart in place. Set up the Lyle gun. Turn over the faking box to release the line. Shovel a deep hole for the sand anchor and then bury it. Hook up the traveling block that carries the breeches buoy. Help Pa set up the crotch to keep the line high above the waves. Pull people to safety.

But I'm not even at the shelter getting ready for survivors. Instead, I'm stranded in the cottage of the two people on Whisper Island who have the least use for me. All because of Mr. Poston.

Miz Aurelia hasn't seemed to notice that we're in the room until she looks up from her boots. "Oh! I thought Sister was here." She looks around the room as if she suspects we've hidden Miz Hortense. "Where is she? What's happened to her? Why are you here? What's wrong with Mr. Poston?"

Questions spill out of her fast and heavy like the rain pouring down outside. I have questions of my own for Miz Aurelia. Where has she been? What's she doing out in a storm like this? Then I notice the hammer she's put down on the bench. That skinny little woman must have been out making sure the Lavender shutters are tight against the storm while her hefty sister remains inside, safe and dry.

Instead of waiting for my answers, Miz Aurelia hurries in to her sister. Her shrill voice cuts the air. "Sister, are you all right? Everything's buttoned up just fine now. Don't you worry. We'll be safe and snug. The storm's bound to blow over any minute."

She sounds like she's talking to a little child instead of a mean-spirited grown woman. Ignoring her chatter, I set about making Mr. Poston more comfortable. I take a wool throw from the bench and cover him. What else? I remember Mama Lu's belief that sugary tea is calming. A kettle simmers on the back of the stove, and I find tea and a pot on the shelf above. I put them all to use.

"Thank you." The little man takes a sip of the hot drink.

I pour a mug for myself and stand close to the fire to warm up and dry my clothes a bit before I set off for the shelter. Surely the sisters will let an injured man stay here until it's safe to go outside.

Before I can be sure of this, someone yells and then bangs on the door.

"Open up!"

THIRTY-SEVEN

caterwaul—*a shrill howl or wail*

In the dim light, I make out my brother Jacob standing on the doorstep. Next to him, a woman as large and tall as Miz Hortense sobs fiercely. A plump girl about my age clutches the woman's wet, torn skirt.

Jacob doesn't seem to notice that I'm not where I should be. "Let us in, Primmy," he shouts over the wind and pounding rain. "We got the captain's wife and daughter off the ship first. They're soaked through and weary."

I motion them in. Before I can ask him what I'm to do next, Jacob disappears. My hopes of helping out at the rescue center disappear with him.

"Oh, dear!" the woman moans. "All my beautiful dresses. My precious jewelry! Ruined! Gone!" She looks ready to collapse, so I settle her on the bench.

Her daughter stands to one side, still gripping her mother's dress. She shivers so forcefully that I wonder why her mother doesn't seem concerned. She can buy herself new clothes, but where could she purchase a new child?

I pry the girl's fingers from her mother's dress and hope she doesn't notice my own trembling.

"Come sit by the fire."

Her wide brown eyes peer at me through straggles of black hair. Sand is caught in the wet tangles, and blowing sand has left red scratches on her arms and face. She looks at her mother, who continues **caterwauling** about her lost finery.

I take the girl's arm. "I'm Primmy Hopkins. What's your name?"

"Claudine," she whispers. "Claudine Leftwich."

I settle her on a rug near Mr. Poston, whose foot looks more swollen. He's somehow managed to fall asleep in the rocking chair. I wish I could so handily escape the storm.

I offer Claudine a soft woolen shawl. Her shivers ease somewhat as she pulls the wrap close around her shoulders. She offers me a weak smile. "Thank you."

"Who was at the door?" Miz Aurelia steps in from the other room. She's changed to dry clothes, and her gray hair hangs in a long braid. She stops short when she sees the two strangers who've fetched up to join Mr. Poston and me.

I explain that her new visitors are from the shipwreck.

She sinks into a barrel chair near the door. "No, no. Sister will be upset. They must leave."

This throws me into a panic. The Life-Saving Service has entrusted me with the care of these survivors. I won't take them out into the deadly weather raging around us. I can't lead them to more safety than we have right here.

I've had about enough of all this concern about Miz Hortense. I stand up straight. "Miz Aurelia, these folks have just been pulled off a wreck. They're cold—"

Earsplitting thunder interrupts me. The cottage shakes, causing the women to screech. Mr. Poston jerks awake and looks wildly around, as if trying to determine where he is and why.

I shout over the shrieks. "They're chilled to the bone. Drenched clear through. Scared. How can you think of turning them out?"

"It's . . . it's just that Sister is so afraid of storms."

I can't picture Miz Hortense afraid of anything, much less storms that are part of island life.

Miz Aurelia goes on. "When she was three, she wandered off one morning, following a stray cat. A storm came up, and she hid in a shed with the cat. The wind tore off the roof and one wall and took the cat with it. Sister never got over it."

"Aurelia Lavender!" Miz Hortense bellows from the other room. "Don't be telling stories on me."

Miz Aurelia squeezes her shoulders in toward her neck. She appears even scrawnier, with nothing but skin and cloth to cover her bones. "I'm—I'm sorry, Sister. I was just explaining why we're not able to be of assistance."

"Stop!" Miz Hortense comes to the doorway. Her face is pale as a fish belly, except for red blotches around her cheeks and eyes. Her hair has come loose from its pinnings. She looks around the room and then fixes on me. "You've no need to explain anything just because Primrose Hopkins wants to open a rescue center here."

I long to argue that I've no intention of asking wreck victims to recover in her unwelcoming cottage. But I'm silent. I've learned that none of my words mean anything to Miz Hortense Lavender.

Lightning flashes in through cracks in the shutters and thunder booms again. Shouts from the beach add to the storm's racket. I strain to hear the words, but the wind's noise muffles them. Miz Hortense screams and retreats into the other room. Her sister follows.

Aside from the fact that she's a woman, Hortense Lavender could never be a surfman. If a ship wrecked during a storm, she couldn't run and hide in her bedroom.

Life-Savers go out no matter how dangerous or rough the storm. Their job is to save people, and that's what they do.

I try to push away thoughts of what bad storms can do, but old-timer stories creep in. Storms have washed across the island, taking away houses and animals—and, worst of all, people. I hope the Lavenders have a trap door to release the pressure of rising water, but I don't see sign of one. If the tide grows high enough, the cottage could easily wash away. And us with it.

These thoughts cause my heart to pound like the surf crashing onto the shore. I swallow down my fright. Worry and fear won't keep the storm away. It's time to take charge of these foolish grown-ups.

I brew more sweet tea and move an armchair to face the fireplace. "Miz Leftwich, sit here. The warmth will help."

She sits close to the fire and sips the hot drink, but her shivers grow worse. Rattling coughs shake her. She could do with a dose of sugar and turpentine and warm, dry clothing. I lead her across the room.

Another crash of thunder shakes the cottage. My stomach knots. Claudine's mother clutches me and coughs. I clench my fist and open the door. "Miz Hortense?"

"Go away!"

"Miz Leftwich needs dry clothes." I push the shaking woman into the next room and close the door.

Rain and rising surf slap against the house. I wonder how high the water has come. Sometimes people move to their upstairs when the water threatens, but this cottage is like ours: all on one floor. I've heard that Mr. Pepperdine and his wife once climbed onto their roof during a storm. They clung to the chimney until the water went down.

There's no hope of my getting these people up on a roof!

Shrieking wind and the clatter of rain against the roof mixes with the surfmen's shouts as they go about their work. The storm pounds rubble against the house. Each pop and crack sends new shivers through me. Being shut up makes every sound seem dangerous and threatening.

Claudine stirs from her place by the fire. Her dress is mostly dry, but tangles of dark hair still cling to her face. She looks toward the other room with a frown. "Mama's sick. Her cough is worse than ever."

As if to prove her right, several hacking coughs rumble from the other room. Deeper and louder than before.

My belly adds another unwelcome sound to remind me that everyone must be hungry. A search through the cupboard shelves turns up a half loaf of brown bread and a round of cheese. A basket of apples sits under the bench by the door. I move everything to the table and brew more tea. The firewood box is nearly empty.

Drat! No matter how much I dread going out into the storm, we need wood.

I knock on the door to the other room. "Miz Aurelia, is your woodshed stocked? We're near out of fire wood."

The door cracks open a bit, and Miz Aurelia peeks out. "I filled it last week." She closes the door before I can say another word. I pull on her storm gear and take a lantern.

"I'm going for more wood," I tell Mr. Poston and Claudine. "There's food on the table. Help yourself."

Neither one moves.

I step out into the storm. Stay close to the cottage wall. Slit my eyes against the stinging rain. Edge around the corner and move away from the wall's shelter. Struggle to avoid slipping on the fallen, drenched leaves. I yank the shed door open, gather an armload of wood, and carry the stack to the cottage. I make two more trips.

When I round the corner with my third load, the front door stands open. Wind pushes rain and flyaway sand inside the cottage. Claudine sags against the doorframe, wringing her hands.

"Mama's gone!"

THIRTY-EIGHT

frazzled—*worn out*

Gone? Has Claudine's mother died while I gathered wood? My stomach knots at the thought. I hang the lantern on its hook. Drop my load of wood on the floor. It takes all my strength to push Claudine aside and shove the door closed against the wind.

She grabs my arm. "Mama took it in her head to run off. Without a wrap or shoes. Please get her back!"

I groan at what's fallen to me. Rescue a crazed woman who's already been rescued. Go back out in the storm. Risk my own life to mayhap save hers. My fists clench in anger, and my cheeks burn.

"Please!" Claudine doubles over with sobs. Her panic breaks my resolve.

"All right. Hold a lamp in the window to guide us."

I snatch up my lantern and push myself back into the wild night. The storm blows in from the ocean. Fights me at every step. I see the troubled woman flinging herself along the beach. She stumbles toward the water. Waves her arms frantically. Veers wildly in one direction and then another.

Struggling against the wind, I finally get close enough to hear her ramblings.

"My clothes. My jewels! Grandmama's brooch! Those men are after my treasures."

I stop alongside to grab her arm, but she swings away so sharply that I fall onto the sand, face-first. I spit out a mouthful of wet grit.

"I must rescue my things before they're all stolen." Her sobs mix with violent coughs as she lurches away.

I run after her. Step right into her path. "We have to go back to the cottage! The ship is sinking. There's nothing left!"

She punches my shoulder hard, and I fall onto my rump. The wind and rain pummel me. I'm ready to lie down on the sand. Let the storm carry me off. I'm done trying to save someone who doesn't want to be saved.

Miz Leftwich reels off. "Stay away from me. You're in with the rest of them. Trying to steal my valuables."

No use trying to force her toward the cottage. She's twice my size and out of her head to boot. I pull myself upright and start after her again with a new scheme. "Miz Leftwich, I'll help you find the ship."

She stops. Stares at me. Nods.

I slowly turn her away from the ocean. I point to the cottage window, where Claudine holds a lantern. "See the light? That's the ship."

As if I'm a herding dog, I guide her toward the cottage. Lightning streaks across the sky, followed by booming thunder. I work hard to keep my charge in tow.

Suddenly, she laughs wildly. Tries to run toward the light. Slips. Slides backwards. Falls down, coughing all the while.

Now I'm sorely rankled. I'll never haul this bulk of a woman to her feet.

"Let's crawl to the ship," I shout over the thunder. "We'll take those men by surprise."

More crazy laughter at my suggestion brings on another coughing fit. She hoists herself to her hands and knees. I crawl alongside. The heavy lantern weighs me down. We slog through the wet sand, fighting the rain. Every inch forward seems to end in five back.

Suddenly she screams. "My leg!"

Drat! What now? I crawl near for a closer look. Holding the lantern over her, I see that a broken shell is stuck just above her knee.

She screams nonstop. I long to slap some sense into

her but think better of it. She could easily send me reeling. Or choke me.

"Here. Let me pull it out. Steady now." I grab the shell and yank. It comes free easily.

Her screams give way to sobs.

I try to comfort her. "It's just a bit farther to the ship. Can you make it?"

"Help me." She flops one arm over my back and leans hard.

It's a struggle to breathe, much less move the two of us toward the house. Unable to hold on to the lantern, I let it tumble to the sand. Thank heaven we're close to the cottage.

Finally we're at the door. Claudine flings it open.

Somehow her mother pulls up and rushes through the doorway. "Where are my treasures?"

I push in behind her and bolt the door. I steady myself on the bench to take off the oilskin gear and try to stop shaking. There's still work to do.

It tests my last bit of strength to help Claudine move her mother to the bedroom door. I knock.

"What do you want now?" Hortense Lavender shouts. "I've had enough of these intrusions. Let us be."

I leave my manners at the door and barge in. "Miz Leftwich must lie down. Her cough needs dosing, and she's cut her leg. Her clothes are wet and—"

"Just look at what she's done to my dress. Torn and bloody. She'll not have another!"

This is too much. "Miz Lavender, you've no call to be so mean. This lady has been through a shipwreck. Lost her clothes. Her jewelry."

The hefty Lavender rants on. "That's nothing to do with me!"

"It's *everything* to do with you and all of us on this island. We have to help one another, stranger or neighbor."

The other Lavender steps forward. "Primmy's right."

"*What?*" Miz Hortense whirls around to stare at her twin.

Miz Aurelia holds her ground. "It's the only way islanders survive. Now find Miz Leftwich another dress. Primmy, help me tend to her."

It's hard to say who is more shocked at this outburst—Hortense Lavender or me. We both follow Miz Aurelia's bidding.

Claudine helps me work the wet, tattered clothes off her mother, who sits limp and miserable.

"Where are my treasures?" she mumbles.

"They're safe, Mama," Claudine whispers.

Coughs jerk her mother as we pull on dry clothes.

"Sugar and turpentine's there." Miz Aurelia points to a brown bottle on the dresser.

My hand shakes as I get a spoonful down Claudine's mother. She sputters at the taste, but it seems to calm her cough. I wash out her cut with soapy water and wrap it in a strip from one of Miz Aurelia's worn petticoats.

Finally, we help the unhappy woman onto the large bed by the far wall and pile on blankets and a quilt. She's asleep before we finish. I long to crawl in beside her and let the storm rage on without me. My legs go soft, and the room seems to spin.

I feel arms holding me up. "Steady," Miz Aurelia says. "You've done a man's work. Saved that poor woman's life. Time to rest and eat."

We leave Claudine's mother to rest. Miz Hortense stays put, arms crossed, face angry.

Her sister heats the kettle while Claudine helps Mr. Poston hobble to the table. I join them, and the four of us eat in silence. We're all too **frazzled** to speak. Soon Mr. Poston goes back to his chair. Claudine curls up on her rug, and Miz Aurelia lies down on the bench. Snores from the bedroom interrupt the quiet.

I settle in an armchair and consider all of us brought together by the storm. We're safe. Warm. Fed. Tended to.

This seems a good time to pray, but last Sunday's sermon slips into my mind. *Have I forgiven everyone?* The person who grieves me most sleeps in the next room.

Now that I know reasons for Miz Hortense's behavior, I mayhap can forgive her rudeness.

I pray for her first, to show my good intentions. Next I ask that everyone in this cottage come through the night unharmed.

"Make sure Pa and Jacob and all the surfmen are safe as well as everyone from the ship.

"Guide Edwin home safe.

"Heal Mr. Poston's ankle. And Miz Leftwich's cough.

"Watch over Mama Lu. And Will and Rowena. Emory and Aunt Marcelle. Elspeth and her ma. Herr Bachmeier. Reverend and Miz Sewell.

"Keep Pansy and all the island critters secure.

"May Mr. Pepperdine and his store come through undamaged.

"Bless every single person on Whisper Island. Amen."

After a spell, I add one more prayer. "Wherever she is, keep my mother happy and safe. Amen.

"And please remind her to write to me.

"Amen again."

THIRTY-NINE

cantankerous—*ill-tempered; irritable*

M iz Lavender!" Loud bangs follow the shout. Startled awake, I wonder why I'm in a chair and not my bed. It comes to me in a flash, and I look around. My three companions are still here. And safe.

Another bang—louder this time—wakes everyone, including the two women in the bedroom.

"Who's pounding outside now?" Miz Hortense shouts from the doorway. "For heaven's sakes, girl, let them in."

Though I long to snap that I'm not her servant, the fight's gone out of me. I'm too weary from yesterday's mishaps to bother arguing. Easier to do what she says. I drag myself out of my chair and shuffle to the door.

Between the bangs and shouts, I hear something

else. Silence. Silence! No wind or thunder. No crashing ocean surge.

I open the door to a calmer day. The air is warm. Sunny patches shine through the clouds, making the wet leaves sparkle. Storm winds have shifted the sand, leaving grit and rubble to cover the cottage doorstep. Surf turned brown with stirred-up sand still pounds the shore.

Justice Sperry and Matthew Stiles stand on the path. Patches of dried muck cling to their Life-Saver uniforms. Dark circles ring their eyes. "Morning, Primmy. Your pa sent us," Emory's pa says. His voice sounds plumb worn out.

"Come in, Mr. Sperry."

"We're here to fetch Miz Leftwich and her girl."

Matthew chimes in. "Everyone's off the ship and safe."

Miz Leftwich limps in from the bedroom. She's a sight. Tangled brown hair. Red-rimmed eyes. Squeezed into another of Miz Hortense's old dresses. She squints at the men. "Josiah has been rescued?"

"Yes, ma'am. He's resting at the Life-Saving Station with his crew. They're all fine, but the ship is lost."

"What about my clothes? Did you save them?"

The two surfmen look hard at each other. Justice Sperry says, "Sorry, ma'am. Our job is to save all the people from a wrecked ship. No matter the cost."

Miz Leftwich's sigh brings on another coughing spell.

As I fetch the cough syrup for the ungrateful woman, I recite the surfmen's motto loud enough for her to hear: "Rule book says we gotta go out, but it don't say nothin' about coming back." It makes no impression on the captain's wife. I give her a hearty dose. She about chokes, but her cough goes quiet.

Mr. Sperry clears his throat. "Primmy, your pa sent us to move the two women over to Miz Lucinda's house. They'll stay there until a ship comes for the captain and his crew."

I smile. We'll soon be freed from this house!

Claudine and I push her mother's feet into a pair of Miz Hortense's waders. We change the dressing on her leg and bundle her up in a quilt to help calm her shivers.

"We're ready," I say.

"What about me?" Mr. Poston bleats. He looks worried that he might be left behind with the Lavenders. I understand his concern.

Justice Sperry answers. "Will and Emory will be along soon. They'll take you to my cottage. Marcelle will take good care of you. She's nursed many a cowboy in her day."

Before we can take one more step, Miz Hortense blocks our way. "What about my ruined dresses?"

Miz Aurelia moves close enough to bite her twin's nose. "Glory, Sister. Don't tell me you're going to be **cantankerous** about clothes. You've got a wardrobe full. More'n any one woman has need of." She takes the captain's wife by the arm and helps the men lead her outside. Claudine and I follow.

Before we turn onto the path for home, I look to see what the storm left on the beach. Broken shells and seaweed litter the sand, along with leavings from the shipwreck—lumber pieces, clothing, crates. I wonder how our village has fared. Are cottages still standing? Did the rescue shelter come through unharmed?

Far out from shore, the wrecked ship's skeleton lies broken in the water, one mast the only part in view.

Claudine pulls my arm. "Papa was so proud to sail that ship. He must be sore unhappy now. I hope he got Matey to land safe."

We walk carefully along the path, stepping over fallen limbs and slipping on the wet mushy leaves. The ground feels like a drenched sponge. It's slow going, but we catch up with the others.

Claudine's mother starts coughing again, and I wish I'd brought along Miz Aurelia's mixture.

"Just a bit farther on, ma'am," Mr. Sperry says.

A few minutes later, we're at Mama Lu's. She comes

to the door with Emory's aunt, and they settle the big woman in a rocker by the fire.

Mama Lu takes over. "Miz Leftwich? I'm Lucinda Tate. This is my friend Marcelle Hoover. Sorry you had to go through such an ordeal."

Miz Leftwich brightens at the sympathy. "Oh, it was terrible. I've lost all my clothes and jewelry."

Mama Lu ignores this and turns to Claudine. "You must be the captain's daughter. Primmy, take her to see the surprise behind the sewing machine."

A chorus of tiny *mews* leads us to a basket filled with kittens. We find Mildred nursing the litter. Mortimer stands guard, and I'm amazed when he lets Claudine hold him in her lap.

After we get Miz Leftwich settled, Emory's aunt hurries off. "I'd best get home to lay out some clothes for Mr. Poston."

Claudine curls up with Mortimer and his new family while Mama Lu and I make breakfast.

Miz Leftwich sighs. Coughs. When we serve up a platter of fried eggs, ham, and Mama Lu's brown bread, she shakes her head. "None for me."

She doesn't bother to say "thank you" or "sorry you went to all that trouble."

Claudine makes up for her mother's rude behavior. Her clothes are bedraggled and stained, but her appetite

and manners are in place. "This is delicious! Thank you."
She reaches for more bread and her third slice of ham.

When she goes back to her post by the cats, I help
Mama Lu clear away the table.

"Primmy!" Will and Emory shout from the gate.

"Hey." I open the door. "Come on in."

"Can't right now," Emory says. "We're on our way to
get Mr. Poston."

But Will comes partway up the path to Mama Lu's
front door. I step down from the porch to meet him.

Will smiles and gives me a loose hug. "I'm mighty
glad you made it through safe. We weren't sure where
you took shelter. I feared for you."

His hug discomfits me, but I'm somehow pleased that
I've caused him worry. "I'm glad too, Will. It was a bad
storm, but it could have been worse."

Will agrees. "It all of a sudden changed directions
and moved on. We were lucky."

I nod. "Did the storm hit the shelter?"

"Herr Bachmeier told Ma this morning that everything stayed put. He's busy today dealing with the ship
captain, but he said to come to the shelter tomorrow to
help set things up for the vendue."

"I'll be there," I promise.

But when I finally wake up, I'm stiff and sore, with a
deep cough in need of Miz Aurelia's sugar and turpentine.

FORTY

fusty—*rotten-smelling*

I wake with a fuzzy head. Between coughs, my mouth feels stuffed with cotton. Cotton that tastes like fish gone bad. In my own bed with no memory of how I got here, I feel as if I'd slept a month away. I'm still in over-alls and one of Edwin's old shirts. They don't smell much better than my mouth.

I struggle to sit up and shrink back with a loud moan.

"She's awake!" Pa's voice booms from the other side of the curtain. He pushes it aside. "Good morning, girl. How do you feel?" He lays his hand on my forehead and turns to Mama Lu, who stands behind him. "Fever seems gone, Lucinda."

Mama Lu steps forward to check for herself. She

touches her cheek to mine and agrees. She smiles. "Ready for some broth, Primmy?"

I consider the taste in my mouth. The stink of my clothes. Hungry as I am, a good washing-up is my first concern. I tell her so.

She nods. "I'll heat up water for a sponge bath. That and clean clothes will make you feel like new."

Though I doubt that, I say nothing. I'm so glad to be home that she could scrub me down in Pansy's watering trough and I'd be happy.

Pa pats my shoulder. "Lie back and rest while you wait. You had a heavy task getting Miz Leftwich in out of that storm. More'n most girls your age would undertake."

His mix of *task* and *undertake* reminds me of school lessons about Greek mythology. A king named Sisyphus committed terrible crimes. For punishment, he had to push a boulder up a hill only to see it roll back down. Just like my ordeal with Miz Leftwich—without the terrible crimes.

It's little wonder that I'm stiff and sore or that I have a **fusty** odor and a bad cough. If I still need a cure, I prefer a dose of Mama Lu's special syrup. She sweetens castor oil and lemon juice with enough brown sugar to make it tolerable.

Minutes later, she brings a basin of hot water. I wash, towel off, and reach for my school shirtwaist.

"Company'll be here soon, Primmy."

Company? Mama Lu doesn't use that word for every-day visitors. Who might be coming?

Before I can ask, she points to my new dresses. "Why not wear one of these?"

I'd forgotten all about them. Haven't worn either since church a week ago. They hang on wall pegs next to my bookcase. The colorful Persian pickle seems to sparkle in the sun coming through my window. The blue dress with its lace collar looks proper and ladylike. An idea comes to me, and I ask Mama Lu her opinion.

She smiles. "Mighty sweet thought, Primmy."

I button up the Persian pickle and give my hair a good brushing. Then I pull back the curtain and hobble my way to the table, like a stiff-legged cripple. "I'm about starved!"

Edwin gives out with a loud guffaw. "Looks like our ol' Primmy is back!" He pulls out a chair for me.

It feels good to hear my brother's teasing.

Pa sits across the table, and Edwin's at my side. Mama Lu sets a dish of broth in front of me. "See how this goes down afore you start on something heavier."

She's simmered a chicken with sage and parsley. I sip the rich, tasty broth and breathe in its hearty aroma. The hot liquid loosens my chest. Brings on a few scattered coughs.

Mama Lu smiles. "You sound a heap better. I 'spect you're on the mend."

No mention of hateful syrup!

"I feel fine." I ask for more broth. Bread and cheese to go with it.

When I finish, Pa stands up. "Glad you feel better, Primmy. I've got business with Gus and Captain Leftwich. Be back soon." Edwin follows him out the door.

I go outside to watch them down the path. Blue skies and bright sunshine greet me. I take in a big gulp of cedar-sweet air. And I cough.

"Sounds like you need dosing!" Will lopes up to our gate. Emory's close behind.

I make a face. "My cough is better."

Will grins. "It should be. You been sleeping since day before yesterday."

My mouth drops open. Two whole days have passed by without me.

"Yep," Emory agrees. "You been hi-ber-nat-in' like a bear." He explodes into laughter.

Will leaves Emory and comes to the porch. "Sure is good to see you up and about."

"Did I really sleep that long, Will?"

He nods. "You dozed off at Mama Lu's. When Edwin got back, he carried you home. Said you were so tuckered out that he put you in your bed, clothes and all. I guess you slept clear through to this morning."

My face burns. I fell asleep in front of Claudine and her mother. When Pa saves someone, he can't go home to rest. He has to be on duty every hour of every day.

Will touches my arm. "You look mighty pretty in that dress, Primmy."

I twist a piece of my hair. "Thank you." Good thing he didn't see—or smell—me an hour ago!

"I bet Claudine doesn't own anything so fine," he says.

Claudine? How does he know anything about her?

"She's staying at Elspeth's house." He grins. "The Leftwich family's spread all over Whisper Island. The captain and Matey are staying with Herr Bachmeier. And when Miz Leftwich heard there was a store on the island, she made her husband take her to Pepperdine's yesterday."

Emory steps up on the porch. "She fainted dead away as soon as she walked in. The Pepperdines been caring for her at their place."

I suspect she thundered to the floor when she realized that Pepperdine's wasn't a fancy, citified shop. Just a general store with flour and nails and a pickle barrel.

While I'm having unkind thoughts about Claudine's ma, Elspeth appears around the bend in the path. She carries the Graces game from the shelter. She turns and motions to someone behind her. "Come on, Claudine."

The captain's daughter shuffles up to the porch. She's stuffed into a faded gingham dress. I recognize it from the stack of clothes we collected for the rescue shelter. It's too snug and too long. A worn belt keeps it from dragging on the ground. Claudine grins when she sees me.

"How are you feeling? We were worried about you, the way you dropped off to sleep."

"I'm doing real good, Claudine." I remember my manners. "How's your ma?"

"She's resting today. Elspeth and I just came from visiting her. She'll be all right, but she's still going on about her lost treasures."

Elspeth about nods her head clean off her neck in agreement.

Claudine hitches up her skirt and bunches it over the frayed belt. "Your dress is really pretty."

Her ill-fitting clothes and kind words decide me. I open the door. "Come inside. I have a surprise for you."

Elspeth and the two boys are about to follow. I hold up my hand and usher Claudine through the doorway. "You three wait out here. We'll just be a minute."

Mama Lu's at the table, peeling apples. She looks up and smiles as we pass by.

In my bedroom, I lift the blue dress from its peg. My reticule slips off with it.

Claudine picks it up, her eyes big. "My mother had one just like this."

I consider the reticule—a gift from my mother. I almost gave it to the shelter, thinking it would lift some lady's spirits. Would it make Miz Leftwich feel better? I'm not sure, but I am certain what I can do for her daughter.

I hand Claudine the dress. "For you. Try it on."

"Oh, Primmy, it's beautiful!"

It's a perfect fit. For once I'm happy to be "pleasingly plump," as Pa would say.

A few minutes later, we step outside.

Three jaws drop open. Will and Elspeth stare, but Emory's smile matches Claudine's.

"Glory! It's just like Cinderella, when the fairy godmother brought her that fancy get-up."

Claudine spins around and around, a whirl of blue. "Thank you, Primmy. It's the prettiest dress I've ever had. And the best surprise."

Will looks at me. Grins.

"You've got some surprises coming too, Primmy."

FORTY-ONE

good some—*very good*

Sssh!" Elspeth scolds Will. "You'll ruin it."
Before Will can reply—before I can ask questions—
Elspeth holds up her Graces game. "Come on, Claudine."

They stand a short distance from each other. Elspeth
crosses the two sticks inside the ribbon-covered hoop,
pulls the sticks apart, and sends the ring flying. Claudine
catches it on her sticks, then shoots it back.

"I want a turn," Emory says.

"Humph!" Elspeth crosses her arms. "Yesterday you
said it was a sissy girl's game!"

"Yep," Emory admits. "It sure looks easy."

Claudine hands her sticks to Emory.

He misses the hoop three times in a row. He's ready
for another turn when Pa strides up the path with Herr

Bachmeier. Edwin follows, along with a tall, burly man who leads the biggest dog I've ever seen. The man wears one of Pa's old shirts. His bald head shines in the sun. As if to make up for this lack of hair, his chin is covered with a thick, black beard.

Claudine runs out to the gate and hugs the stranger.

All four men smile at me. The dog wags his tail. His slobber makes wet circles on the sandy path.

"*Guten Morgen, Klöbchen.*" Herr Bachmeier tips his hat. "I am glad to see you in good health."

"*Danke.*"

Pa introduces me to the newcomer. "Captain Josiah Leftwich."

"'Morning, sir. Pleased to meet you."

"Pleased to meet you as well, Primmy. I'm grateful to you for getting my wife, Iola, to safety. You're a mighty brave young woman."

I marvel at how grown folks keep putting the word *woman* on me.

Mama Lu comes out to join us by the gate. She puts her arm around my shoulder and gives me a squeeze.

The captain goes on. "Mrs. Leftwich is somewhat indisposed right now, but I'm sure if she could be here, she'd thank you in person."

I doubt that. That woman's too selfish to think of showing gratitude.

As if she could read my thoughts, Mama Lu pinches my arm.

It's a *mind-your-manners* pinch. I oblige. "I hope she feels better real soon."

Edwin speaks up. "Primmy's brave *and* strong, sir. Takes care of Pa and me and Jacob all by herself. Cooks, cleans, washes our clothes. Even tends to my pig Pansy." He winks at me. "And hardly ever complains."

My face burns so fierce that I think the fever's back.

The captain clears his throat. "I can never repay you for your kindness and bravery, but I can give you a new friend." He looks down at the dog. "Matey here just took his first ocean voyage. I don't think he'll ever willingly set his paws on a ship again after going through the wreck. It would be cruel to force the sea upon him. I'd like to leave him with you, Primmy. From what I hear, you'll give him a good home."

I stare at him. Then at Matey, who studies me with sad brown eyes.

I pat his head, and he nuzzles against me.

"Can I take him, Pa?" I ask.

He laughs. "Well, we'll have to lay in extra food for such a big critter, but I reckon his company will be well worth it."

I don't know where to put my hug first—on Pa or Matey or Captain Leftwitch. I settle on Matey. He sits back on his haunches and pushes into my arms.

The captain rumples the dog's thick brown-and-white fur. "Looks like you've got yourself a new friend!"

Everyone crowds around my dog and me.

Claudine does another whirl in her blue dress. "Papa, look what Primmy gave me. Isn't it pretty?"

"It surely is. Very nice of you, Primmy."

"She's got a reticule, too, exactly like the one you gave Mama for Christmas."

The captain sighs. "My darling Iola surely did love that reticule. She carried it everywhere. Kept her best jewelry inside. She even grabbed it up before I could get her off the ship."

I question the idea of Miz Leftwich being anyone's "darling." Mama Lu reads my thoughts. Pinches again. Harder.

"We found no sign of a purse when we unhitched her from the breeches buoy," Pa says. "Probably dropped into the water."

Herr Bachmeier steps forward. "We will look for it. If it washes ashore, I give my word as Wreckmaster that we will return it to your wife."

"I'd be much obliged," the captain says.

Their words mix in with my thoughts. Should I offer Claudine's mother my fancy purse to make up for her loss? It's not as if I'll ever use it. I never wanted it in the first place, and it might cheer Miz Leftwich.

My pondering ends when Jacob rushes up the path, along with Justice Sperry and Emory's aunt. "Are we too late, Pa?"

"Naw, you're just in time." Pa steps up on the porch. Claps his hands. "I've official business to conduct here, ladies and gentlemen. Give me your attention."

We fall silent and look at Pa.

He clears his throat. "Primrose Estella Hopkins has performed life-saving duties with bravery and without any thought to her own safety. In recognition of her outstanding performance, she will be awarded a special citation from the United States Life-Saving Service."

Everyone claps.

Pa turns to me. "Primmy, I'm real proud of you. We all are." His hug about squeezes the stuffing out of me.

"Say a few words," Edwin yells. "Speechify, Primmy."

More clapping. Then silence. Everyone looks at me.

I twist my skirt. Tug at my hair. "Not much I can say, other than 'thank you.' I appreciate getting an award, but I didn't do more than what any of you would've done. Thank you."

I try a little curtsy, but my feet tangle and I nearly tumble over. I can just about hear my mother's sigh from across the Sound.

Will catches my elbow. "You're a real hero, Primmy."

"He's right." Pa sweeps his arm toward the rain barrel,

past Pansy's enclosure, across to the patch of marigolds at the edge of the porch. "Everyone here agrees."

Mama Lu believes the events of life often bring lessons when we most need them. I ponder this as I look at our yard crowded with family and friends. Filled with hugging and clapping and laughter. What lessons have recent events brought me?

There are limits to making another person happy. I thought my mother would be happy if I crossed the Sound and met her in Cranston, but I was wrong. I doubt my reticule would bring any real contentment to Iola Leftwich. Like my mother, she'll always want something more.

At times, a person has to find a way around rules and do what needs doing. Though I'm not a proper member of the Life-Saving Service, I *did* save a life. There's no rule to stop me from helping shipwrecked folks at the rescue center.

Some parts of life seem disinclined to change. The Life-Saving Service won't accept a woman in their ranks. Hortense Lavender will never be friendly—leastways not to me. I doubt my mother will ever take me as I am—just plain Primmy.

Most of all, I've learned that this **good some** spot is the best place for me.

Whisper Island.

My home.

Acknowledgments

LIKE MOST BOOKS, *Whisper Island* is the result of the work and wisdom of many people other than the author. First—and always—I'm grateful to my husband, Peter, for his encouragement and support.

I owe much to the dedication of my Wednesday morning critique group. They have cared for and nurtured my telling of Primmy's story and helped me see what was needed to bring her to life.

James and Linda, the devoted keepers of the Chicamacomico Life-Saving Museum, gave freely of their time and enthusiasm to help me share the story of a group of our nation's heroes with young readers.

And, finally, to the brave United States Life-Savers, who put their lives on the line whenever a ship wrecked in coastal waters or along the shores of the Great Lakes. Their story is indeed worth remembering.

Thank you all!

DISCUSSION QUESTIONS

1. Primmy's goal of becoming a United States Life-Saver is impossible for a girl in 1913. How does she come to terms with this fact?

2. Primmy has firm ideas about Elspeth Thornton without really knowing her. How and why do those ideas change? Why do you think people form ideas about someone they don't really know?

3. Her mother left when Primmy was three. How has that affected her? How would Primmy's life be different if her mother had stayed on the island?

4. How does her trip to Cranston affect Primmy? What does she learn about herself? About her mother? Does anything good come from the trip?

5. Some characters present real difficulties for Primmy. How does she meet the challenge of Hortense Lavender? Of Iola Leftwich? Of Mr. Poston?

6. Although she often makes careless mistakes, what actions throughout the book show that Primmy is capable and strong?

7. How does Primmy's relationship with Will change in the book?

8. How does Primmy feel when she tries on the dresses Mama Lu has made for her? How does she feel about the new clothes her mother gives her? Why do you think she keeps the reticule for herself, even though she gives away the rest of her mother's gifts?

9. What do you think Primmy's relationship with her mother will be like when Primmy is an adult?

10. At the end of the book, Primmy realizes that there are limits to making another person happy. Do you agree? Why?

AUTHOR'S NOTES

THE IDEA FOR *Whisper Island* was sparked by a shipwreck story I heard while visiting the Outer Banks. The 1913 wreck of the George H. Wells caught my fancy because the captain came off the ship in a breeches buoy, carrying his Saint Bernard. He later gave the dog to the Life-Savers who had rescued him, his family, and crew. When I learned that women were not allowed to serve as Life-Savers, I knew I had a problem for a spunky girl to overcome. I named her Primrose Estella and gave her a personality completely unlike her fancy name. She's just plain Primmy.

These Outer Banks are often called "The Graveyard of the Atlantic" because thousands of ships have wrecked along that stretch of the Atlantic coast. When you visit the Outer Banks (and I hope you will!), be sure to visit Chicamacomico and the Life-Saving Historic Site and Museum. You'll be able to see a reenactment of the Life-Savers' drill the way it was done in 1913. You'll also have a chance to see all the equipment that Primmy's pa and his crew used to rescue folks. You'll even see a handsome man in full Life-Saver's uniform! However, you won't find a barrier island named Whisper Island. I created it for this book, and I hope it shows how Outer Bankers lived in 1913.

The United States Life-Saving Service (USLSS) was an important part of America's early history. When they went to the aid of a wrecked ship, the men performed difficult, dangerous work. They carried out rescues whenever needed, for very little pay. Their motto, "We have to go out, but we don't have to come back" shows that they were willing to face their own death to save the lives of others. They served in the worst weather conditions: raging storms, crashing waves, and violent wind. The surfmen trained every day and kept watches up and down the beach and in the station's lookout tower. Every Life-Saving station in the United States—along both ocean coasts and the shores of the Great Lakes— followed this work and watch routine.

In 1915, the USLSS became the United States Coast Guard, along with the Revenue Cutter Service. Service did not open to women until 1918, after the United States entered World War I. Twin sisters Genevieve and Lucille Baker were the first uniformed women to serve in the Coast Guard.

There really was a traveling toothbrush salesman who visited the islands in the early 1900s. He sold black-gum twigs, two for a nickel. One end was softened so that it was like a brush. Islanders dipped it in baking soda to brush their teeth. Some continued to use the twigs long after machine-made toothbrushes were available.

Each chapter begins with an "old-timey" word. Some words, such as *meehonkey*, are peculiar to the Outer Banks. To learn more about this language, read *Hoi Toide on the Outer Banks* by Walt Wolfram and Natalie Schilling-Estes. In the book, Emory's father is member of the Whisper Island Life-Saving crew. African-Americans began service in USLSS shortly after the Civil War. In 1879, Richard Etheridge became the first African-American Keeper. His Pea Island crew was entirely African-American and their service record is outstanding.

For more information, visit the following sites:

The US Life-Saving Service
www.uslife-savingservice.org/history_of_the_uslss

The Live-Saving Service Museum
www.chicamacomico.net/

Women in the Coast Guard
www.uscg.mil/history/womenindex.asp

Traveling Salesmen
www.villagecraftsmen.com/news080105.htm

African Americans in the Life-Saving Service
www.navalhistory.org/.../navy-tv-the-story-of-the-pea
-island-lifesavers/

About the Author

Anola Pickett grew up in a family of storytellers. Even her name has a story: it's a combination of her two grand-mothers' names—Ann and Ola. Every family story grew longer and more colorful each time another person told it. In third grade Anola discovered that writing down stories was fun too. In college she combined her love of reading and writing and earned a degree in English and creative writing. After spending several years as an elementary and middle school teacher, Anola worked as a school librarian. Now she writes full-time at her home in Kansas City. A few years ago, she discovered that she enjoys writing historical fiction for young readers.

She and her husband, Peter Doyle, enjoy traveling together and always come back with at least one idea for another story!

You can learn more at www.anolapickett.com.